CUSS

CUSS

Kristine L. Franklin

CANDLEWICK PRESS
CAMBRIDGE, MASSACHUSETTS

Copyright © 2003 by Kristine L. Franklin

First paperback edition 2007
Originally published as *Grape Thief*

Introductory photograph of Roslyn, Washington, circa 1922 courtesy of The Roslyn Museum

Photograph on page 293 courtesy of S. M. Brozovich Collection

The Library of Congress has cataloged the hardcover edition as follows:

Franklin, Kristine L.
Grape thief / by Kristine L. Franklin. —1st ed.
p.   cm.
Summary: In 1925, in a small Washington State community made up of families from different ethnic backgrounds, twelve-year-old Cuss tries to stay in school as he watches those around him struggle with various financial difficulties.
ISBN 978-0-7636-1325-9 (hardcover)
[1. City and town life—Washington (State)—Fiction.
2. Washington (State)—Fiction. 3. Croatian Americans—Fiction.]
I. Title.
PZ7.F859226 Cu 2003
[Fic]—dc21   2002023774

ISBN 978-0-7636-2362-3 (paperback)

2 4 6 8 10 9 7 5 3 1

Printed in the United States of America

This book was typeset in Granjon.

Candlewick Press
2067 Massachusetts Avenue
Cambridge, Massachusetts 02140

visit us at www.candlewick.com

To the memory of my paternal grandparents,
Andrija and Uljana Brozovich,
born subjects of the emperor of Austria and Hungary;
died free citizens of the United States of America

Chapter One

The grape train pulled into Roslyn on a hot
August day in 1925. The air felt like the devil's
breath. My pal Perks and I were up in the hills above
town looking for our cows. The sun made me lazy. It
turned my brain to jelly. That's the only reason I fell
for Perks's prank.

"Hiking in this heat is gonna kill me, Cuss," said
Perks. "I can't take it no more."

"If the cows wander into town, the cow catcher'll
impound 'em," I said, wiping the sweat off my face.
"Last time that happened, Ma had to pay a dime apiece
to get 'em back, and she took it out on my hide."

"There's a way to find cows right off," said Perks,
"but it's magic, so I don't s'pose I can tell you."

"Liar," I said.

"I ain't lying," said Perks. "Swear to God and the Lord Jesus."

"So give over," I said, ready like always for one of Perks's whoppers.

"Swear you won't tell."

"I swear on the grave of my pa," I said, crossing myself to show I was serious. The sun baked my back right through my shirt.

"Good enough," said Perks. "Here's the skinny. If two boys make water on the top of a rock, whichever way it trickles down, that's the exact direction the cows is in. It's surefire. Works with goats, sheep, sometimes even chickens. It's African magic."

"Says who?" I asked.

"Granny," said Perks. "And she got it from Darlin' Auntie Mavis, who was a witch." He leaned close to me and dropped his voice. "Darlin' Auntie boiled the bones off a black cat and sucked the meat from each and every bone until she found the bitter bone that gave her the Sight."

I felt a shiver scurry up my spine. I crossed myself again, this time against evil spirits. Perks looked sincere enough, but still, I wasn't sure I wanted to trust him.

"Some folks are born with the Sight," Perks whispered. "But if you use magic to get it, that makes you a witch."

"Why would anybody tell you witch secrets?" I asked.

"Granny didn't tell me directly," said Perks. "I overheard."

That sounded more like it. I licked my dry lips. If Perks was right, I could be at home, soaking my head under the water pump in no time at all.

"Here's a rock, Cuss," said Perks, pointing to a knee-high boulder lodged in the ground. "Looks like a little mountain. That's the right kind."

The sweat trickled down my back. I checked Perks's face for signs of tomfoolery, but he looked as serious as a nun during Lent.

He nodded toward the rock. "You go first. I'll add my stream to yours directly."

I unbuttoned my overalls and as soon as I had my business in my hand, Perks started to howl with laughter. I felt my ears turn red and buttoned up my pants. Perks pointed at me. He slapped his thighs and hooted. Then he mimicked the look on my face and pretended to button up his own pants.

"You shouldn't pull tricks on your best pal," I said. "Put up your dukes." I took a step backward, tossed my cap aside, pulled back my fist, and got ready to deal him his desserts. Perks grinned and dove for my legs instead. He knocked me to the ground and we tussled for a couple of minutes, rolling in the dirt and pine needles.

I got in some good shots and was just about ready to land a sneak undercut when Perks hauled off and popped me in the schnoz. Blood poured out. Perks saw it and hopped off me, wiping his hands on his shirt.

"I think I broke my hand on that big bohunk nose," he said, kissing his fist. Blood always ended a tussle.

"You win," I said, standing up. Perks danced around like a prizefighter, thumbing his nose and boxing the air. I laughed and kicked some dust in his direction. I picked my cap up off the ground and stuck it back on my head. Then I plugged one side of my nose and blew bloody snot into the dirt. "But you should apologize for lying to me."

"If you say so, Cuss."

"Yeah, I say so."

"Mr. Slava Petrovich," said Perks with a wide smile, "I humbly apologize for pulling a fast one on you, you old sun-muddled bohunk."

"That's more like it," I said. "Next time I might have to rearrange your face."

Perks grabbed his own nose. "No, thanks. I don't want to look like that ugly Snakey."

4

Back in second grade I took on a bully named Snakey who'd called my pa a word in Estonian that I wouldn't repeat in English. Pa'd died from the influenza only a few years before that, and I didn't take too kindly to anyone's smearing his name, not in any language. Maybe Snakey thought all I knew was Croatian. I showed him, even though I was just a squirt. First I called him a big *pōrsas*, meaning "pig," which I'd picked up from one of my brother's Estonian pals, and then—*socko!*—one punch and Snakey was down with a busted nose.

After that I started paying close attention to the other ethnics. I listened to what they said, especially when they were drunk and hollering at each other. I collected their cuss words and insults. Pretty soon they figured out what I was up to and went along with my game. I only had to hear a word once to remember it. They taught me that *joodik* meant "drunkard" in Estonian, and *träskpadda* meant "swamp frog" in Swede, and that *pupa-ma-n* meant "kiss my butt" in Romanian. I told them if I knew enough cuss words in other languages, no kid would ever be able to pull a fast one in Old Country talk. They thought I was a hoot. And they gave me a nickname that stuck: Cuss.

By the end of second grade I could say "You look like a horse's hinder" in Croatian, Turk, Slovenian,

Italian, Estonian, Albanian, Lithuanian, Hungarian, Swede, Finn, Polack, Czech, and even Arab, which I got from Perks, whose Granny knew a Gypsy who shacked up with a guy from Arabia. I knew a lot of other cuss words, too. Guess you could say I had the knack.

"You're bleedin' all over," said Perks. "Your ma's gonna kill you."

"Not likely," I said, wiping my throbbing nose on my shirt. "Ma's used to boys." Perks threw his skinny arm around my shoulder.

"Cuss, your problem is you're too slow. Someday I'll give you a ride in my spankin'-new Ford sedan," he said. "The fastest, slickest, shiniest one off the lot. Then you'll know fast." Perks made the sound of a motorcar. He drove an invisible steering wheel.

"Fat chance you'll ever own a Ford," I said.

"Didn't I tell you?" said Perks. "I'm already smart, and someday I'm gonna be rich, too."

"Smart-*mouthed*," I said. "You got that much right."

"Smart as in *smart*," said Perks. "My grades are as good as yours."

"More lying," I said. "You're gonna flunk out."

"No bohunk in all of history ever got past grade seven," said Perks. "You'd best forget about school and become a mechanic and maybe I'll let you work on my Ford." We both laughed at that. Who ever heard of a white man working for a colored man?

A train whistle blew long and loud down in town. It wasn't the everyday sound of a coal train, and it wasn't the sound of a passenger train. It was the sound of a train that only came to Roslyn once a year.

"Is that what I think it is?" said Perks.

The train whistle blew again and we heard a shout. We turned and saw Skinny Giombetti running toward us up the hill, waving his arms.

Chapter Two

"Perks! Cuss!" yelled Skinny. "I've been looking all over for you knuckleheads. The grape train's here." Skinny was so fat that whenever he ran he got short of breath. "Grapes!" he said, gasping. "The grape train's in town!"

"I can taste 'em already!" said Perks.

"How many boxcars this year?" I asked Skinny. My nose throbbed something awful. I hoped it didn't look as big as it felt. Skinny caught his breath and answered.

"Four," he said. "All full to the brim with tons and tons of big, fat, juicy, ripe Black Bear wine grapes all the way from California. . . . You been fighting?" Before I could answer, Skinny said, "Ma already ordered sixteen boxes, but you can bet four bits I won't get a single one to eat just plain. I love grapes. Juicy grapes, sweet grapes, grapes from the Golden State." He closed his eyes and smiled. Perks elbowed me.

"Your ma bought sixteen boxes? That's three hundred twenty pound of grapes," said Perks, and then he whistled. "You folks oughta drink beer. It's cheaper. Ten cents a bucketful on Saturdays after quitting time."

Skinny shrugged. "We're wops. What do you expect? How many grapes is your ma gonna buy, Cuss?"

"Beats me," I said. *Not as many as the butcher's wife,* I thought to myself. Ma's money always had to go a lot further than the Giombettis', what with them only having Skinny and his plain-Jane sister, Helen, and Ma having all of us. The only wine she made was used for medicine. The train blew its whistle again.

The grape train had been coming to Roslyn ever since Prohibition started five years back. Beer, wine, whiskey, you name it, overnight it was all against the law. Legal or not, the ethnics had to have their wine, and if they couldn't buy it, by golly they'd make it. The California grape farmers were happy to help them out.

There was no finer sensation on earth than a mouthful of Black Bear grapes. They were better than plums or cherries. They came from California, a faraway place boys like us only dreamed about. The sweet grapes popped in our mouths and squirted juice all the way to the backs of our throats. There was nothing like it. But it wasn't only the taste of grapes that grabbed us. It was how we got our hands on them.

Every year the grape train pulled into town, and every year dozens of boys tried to steal grapes. After the first year the railroad company started posting a bull around the clock until all the grapes were sold, but that didn't stop us. We came by night, sneaking and scheming and making off with grapes. It wasn't good enough to pick them up off the ground. You had to snatch whole bunches from the boxcars. That was the trick. My cousins Turk and Putzy held the record so far — one whole box apiece.

The railroad bulls carried nightsticks, so we worked extra hard to steer clear of them. So far, every year me and Skinny and Perks had managed to grab a few bunches out of a boxcar and run. I got a smack on the behind from a nightstick once, but it was worth it. This time I had a plan. I'd been working on it for a whole year.

"Here's the lowdown," I said, and beckoned my pals in close. I whispered my plan to Skinny and

Perks. They laughed and cheered, and Perks did a little dance.

"Swear to secrecy," I said. "Skinny?"

Skinny dug in his knickers pocket and pulled out his black rosary beads, a pocketknife, and a nickel. He shoved the beads and knife back into his pocket and held out the coin. I put the nickel in my hand, buffalo up. Then I hocked a loogie right on it. Skinny spit, and so did Perks. I rubbed the nickel with my thumb and handed it to Perks. He did the same and handed it back to Skinny. Skinny rubbed the nickel, then wiped it off and stuck it back in his pocket.

"Me and Perks have to round up the cows," I said to Skinny. I was loaded with get-up-and-go. There's nothing like a nighttime raid to give a boy ants in his pants. "You check out the particulars."

"Hokey-dokey," said Skinny. He took off his cap and rubbed a hand over the stubble of his summer pig shave. By the first snow his head would be covered with black curls and he'd be trying to straighten them with wax. "Do we meet at midnight, same place as last year?"

"I gotta work," said Perks, "but I'll be there anyhow." Perks's ma ran the colored cafe, which, like all the cafes and soda joints in Roslyn, sold soda pop and ice cream and sandwiches to strangers, bootleg and beer to regulars. Perks worked late every night, except for an occasional Sunday when he got hauled off to a revival meeting at the Colored Baptist Church.

"Try to get there at twelve, straight up," I said.

Skinny yelled, "Yahoo!" Then he turned and ran back toward town. Me and Perks, our arms around each other's shoulders, went to find the cows in the regular way.

Chapter Three

When I got home Ma told me supper would be late and to do my chores beforehand. I should have figured something fishy was going on when Mary paid me a penny to do her milking, but I was too busy plotting and planning and dreaming of grapes to think twice about it. I called Philip and we headed to the barn.

Philip milked Bernice, and I got both Daisy and Geraldine. We brought the milk into the house and set the pails on the counter. Ma strained it into jars and I carried them down into the cellar and set them on the shelf to let the cream rise.

"How come Mary's too busy to milk?" I asked Ma, sticking a finger into the gravy she was stirring on the cookstove. She gave me a quick hug and then she swatted at my hand.

"Get your dirty hands out of my food," said Ma in Croatian. "Is that what they teach you in school, Mr. Smarts?" Sweat poured down her face, but she looked happy. Ma was always happiest when she was cooking, even if it was a hundred degrees outside and twice that hot in the kitchen. "Mary's getting ready," said Ma. "She invited a gentleman for supper."

Ma smiled and winked at me. We had one wedding coming up in just over a month. My brother Matt was engaged to his longtime sweetheart, Emmeline Cimmermancek, and Ma was pleased as punch. At twenty, Mary was practically an old maid. She was pretty enough, as girls go, and she'd had plenty of boys hanging around, but so far nobody had talked her into tying the knot. I wish I'd known there was a fellow involved. I could have charged two cents for milking.

"Is it Hairy?" Hairy Bovitz, so called because he'd gone bald by age seventeen, had been sniffing around our house for months.

"Mary says Clement Bovitz is too ugly," said Ma. She sighed and stirred. "But he works hard and he never misses mass. Hardly ever gets drunk, either. She couldn't do better than that, if you ask me."

"So who is it, then?" I asked. Philip had hopped up on a stool. He was wiggling his front tooth.

"He's a boarder," said Philip. "His name is Mr. Thompson. Philip yanked out the tooth and held the bloody thing up for me to see. "She's really putting on the ritz for him, too. Cuss, did you ever hear of the Tooth Fairy?"

"Nah," I said. "Go feed the pigs. Do something useful instead of getting blood all over the place." Philip hopped down. I smacked him on the behind as he ran out the door. I swiped a carrot from the pile Ma had peeled. She pretended not to notice.

Mary worked washing clothes at the Roslyn Boardinghouse for six cents a pound, dry weight. Not bad for a girl. It was likely her boarder was a run-of-the-mill bachelor miner. Just then Mary sashayed into the kitchen.

"Cuss, you're filthy," she said. She was wearing her church dress, the one with beads sewn onto the front in the shape of flowers. "You look like you've been fighting."

I looked at Ma, who looked at me and frowned. I was never sure how much English she understood. Guess she'd understood that all right. My hand flew to my face and I covered my swollen beak.

"The devil will get you for fighting, Slava," said Ma. "Is that what they teach you in school? If you act like a drunken coal miner you'll grow up to be one, eh? Pray for us, O Holy Mother of God." She shook

15

her head and stirred gravy, but I knew she wasn't mad. Fighting was what boys did for fun.

"My brothers are all such *pigs,*" said Mary.

Just then Philip came in the back door with a piglet in his arms. "Cuss, look," said Philip. "This little pig has a hurt foot." The piglet squealed and struggled in Philip's arms. I looked at its left hind hoof. "It's swollen," said Philip. "I tried sulfur salve—one part sulfur powder, four parts lard, just like always—but it ain't working." It was the same salve that Ma mixed up to smear on us when we had the itch. I scratched the piglet between the ears.

"If it works on boys, it oughta work on a pig, Phil. Give it some time."

The piglet squealed.

"Get that pig out of the house!" cried Mary.

"Take the pig out," said Ma.

"He cut it a week ago," said Philip. "You should see him limp." By now the piglet was squealing so loudly that Philip had to shout. "His tail is sticking straight out, Cuss. He feels hot." Philip turned the piglet around to show me its back end. It wiggled out of his arms, dropped to the floor, and took off at a trot.

"Catch it!" screamed Mary.

Philip grabbed for the pig but missed. I cornered the pig between the stove and the wood box and grabbed it. Ma had turned her back to the whole commotion. I shooed the piglet in Philip's direction. Phil grinned, and the gap in his smile made him look like a jack-o'-lantern. The piglet ran between his legs and we both laughed.

"Mama, this is a *disaster*!" yelled Mary, her voice quivering with rage.

Just then I heard my brother Matt's fine tenor voice over the hubbub. "Be it ever so humble, there's no place like home!" He sang loud and clear just outside the door. The piglet squealed and Philip giggled. Mary tried to hit Philip but missed. Matt stuck his head inside the back door. The pig ran into the sitting room. Philip chased after it. Mary hollered at Philip.

Matt wiped the coal dust from around his mouth, but the rest of his face was black. He still had on his miner's hardhat. It was black, too, covered with coal dust. "Home, sweet home," he said. "A haven, an abode of peace. Smells good, Ma!" Matt's eyes were almost as dark as the coal dust and they sparkled with mischief. He winked at me and rolled his eyes in Mary's direction.

I knew Joey must be with him, too, but he was our quiet brother, the one who watched and listened but hardly ever let on what he was thinking.

"*Philip! Get that pig out!*" yelled Mary. "And don't you boys *dare* come in the house like that. You're *filthy.*"

"Uh-oh," said Matt. "Big sister's got a flea in her corset." He grinned and his teeth shone extra white against the black dirt on his face. "Philly boy," he yelled, "the barn is outside! You'd better scram before Mary takes the broom to your patootie."

"Clean up, all you," said Ma in English. She hadn't turned around. I could see her whole body shaking with laughter. She switched to Croatian. "Take out the pig, Filip."

"Pig?" said Matt, still grinning. "Pig? I thought Mary was singing. Joe, didn't it sound like singing to you?" Matt turned and elbowed Joey, who smiled but didn't say a word.

"Mama!" said Mary. Just then Philip and the pig ran through the kitchen. Matt held open the door and the pig ran out and down the back steps. Matt grabbed Philip and tickled him.

"Baby brother, are you the cause of all this ruckus?" Philip giggled and slugged Matt in the arm. "Ow! You broke my arm!" Matt let him down and Philip hurried off to catch the pig.

"Enough," said Ma, trying hard not to laugh.

"Just dropping off our lunch buckets," said Matt. He set his pail inside the door, and so did Joey, then the two of them set off toward the wash house. Mary left the kitchen in a huff. I grabbed a plum out of a bowl, bit into it, and thought about the grapes I'd be eating that very night. Maybe I'd bring a few for Phil, as long as he'd swear not to tell. I headed out the door.

My brothers were at the wash house. They'd stripped off their mine clothes and were scrubbing the black from their faces and necks and hands.

"How come Mary's in such a tizzy, Cuss?" Matt asked me. He winked and motioned for me to pump water. I pumped the handle up and down.

"Mary's bringing home a fellow," I said. Matt splashed his face and head.

"Lucky Hairy," he said. "I told him not to give up." He scrubbed his big, muscled arms up past the elbows and then splashed his face again. "I don't s'pose I have to shave for old Hairy." He rubbed his afternoon stubble with one hand.

"It ain't Hairy," I said. "It's somebody new in town. A boarder named Thompson." Matt stood up straight and the water poured down his face.

"Oh, yeah?" He looked at Joey.

"Blond guy?" asked Joey. Matt and I both looked at our brother. Joey rarely said two words together. Ever since coming back from the Great War he'd been that way. Matt said it was on account of his eating too much French food. Matt could turn anything into a joke, even the change in Joey.

I shrugged. "Beats me." I pumped water into another basin and splashed my own face. The cold felt good on my nose. I grabbed the yellow block of hard soap and scrubbed my hands.

We finished washing and the big boys got clean clothes off the hooks in the wash house. Ma hollered for us to come to supper and we filed up the path to the house. No one said a word, not even Matt, but I didn't think twice about it. Right then I had grapes on the brain.

Chapter Four

When Mary's boarder friend came up the path, Philip let out a low whistle. "Hell's bells," he said. With that missing tooth, it sounded just like "helth belth." Mary had shooed us out of the sitting room, so we were spying from the window in Ma and Mary's bedroom instead.

Thompson was tall. He had a thick yellow mustache that covered his upper lip, and his skin was brown from the sun. His hair was the color of old straw. When he came up the steps, I saw that his eyes were the same gray blue as the ice we cut up at the pond every winter. He wore real shoes, not boots.

Thompson knocked. Mary answered the front door and invited him in. Philip and I tiptoed across the bedroom. I opened the bedroom door and peeked out. We spied as Mary introduced him to Ma, whose face was like a stone.

"Ma, this is my friend Roger Thompson."

"Pleased to meet you, Mrs. Petrovich," said Thompson. Ma held out her plump hand, but she didn't smile.

"He isn't a Croat," she said in Croatian. "What is he? A Swede? A Finn?"

"English, Ma," said Mary. Her face had turned the color of a ripe huckleberry. Philip started to giggle. I elbowed him to shut up. I didn't want to miss a word.

"English?" said Ma, still in Croatian. "That's worse. The English think they're better than everyone."

"No, I mean *speak* English," said Mary in Croatian.

Philip snorted. No one told Ma what to do, least of all which language to speak when.

Ma looked Thompson up and down, then turned around and went to the kitchen. Mary half smiled and invited Thompson to sit down. Soon they were joined by Joey and Matt. This was going to be grand.

Philip and I got banished to the kitchen because there wasn't enough room at the table for everyone. We sat on stools with our plates in our laps, straining our ears to hear the goings-on in the dining room.

Mary was speaking in English. "Ma, Roger is a businessman."

Ma answered in Croatian. "He should mind his own business."

Mr. Thompson spoke. "Very fine supper, Mrs. Petrovich. Is this one of your own chickens?"

Ma, still speaking Croatian, asked, "Is he a Catholic? Swedes are all Lutherans."

Mary answered Mr. Thompson for Ma in English. "Ma says thank you, yes, it's one of ours, and please have more." Then she said in Croatian to Ma, "Mother, I like him. Please, please don't scare him away."

Ma snorted.

Matt spoke up. "So, Thompson, what sort of business are you in?"

"Mercantile. I'm looking to set up a store here. Farm goods, hardware, household appliances."

"Where are you from?" asked Matt.

"Out east."

Joey spoke in Croatian. "That's him."

Matt answered in Croatian. "You positive?"

"Joseph! Matthew!" exclaimed Mary.

Ma asked in Croatian, "Do you know this Englishman, Yosip?"

Now Mary was frantic. "Roger, tell the boys and Ma about the grizzly bear you shot in Montana."

Thompson started to yammer away about his travels. I was done eating and had found a perch just inside the kitchen door where I could sit and watch. Thompson talked about coming across the states by train. His voice was smooth the way I imagined an actor's would be, easy to listen to, like the low notes of Matt's guitar. Mary never took her eyes away from his face. She had it bad.

Ma started to clear the table, clattering the plates and gathering up the napkins. Mary must've had a screw loose to think Ma would accept this Thompson. Ma was Old Country, bone and marrow, and in the Old Country, you married your own kind.

I watched my big brothers. Joey didn't look up from the table. Matt shifted in his chair, first watching Thompson and then looking over at Joey. Matt started tapping a rhythm with his knife until Ma snatched it out of his hand.

Ma carried a load of dishes into the kitchen. Philip and I crowded by the door. She pushed her way past us as if we weren't there.

"Excuse me for a just a jiffy," Mary said as she jumped up to follow Ma into the kitchen. She smacked me on the shoulder and bopped Philip on the top of his head. "Quit spying, you brats," she said in Croatian.

"Outside, you boys," said Ma. Her head was high. Her jaw was set. We did as we were told. I grabbed the *Miner's Echo* off the kitchen shelf on my way out the back door.

"I'm going to Pinky's house," said Philip, heading down the alley. "His ma is sick, and his sisters make him do extra chores, even ironing." I sat on the back steps and cracked the back door open half an inch. I opened up the paper to read.

"Mama," whispered Mary in Croatian, "I think he wants to propose."

"How long have you known this Thompson? Two days?"

"Longer than that," said Mary. "What does it matter? You never even *met* Pa before you married him!"

"That was different. Our parents chose for us. No daughter of mine is marrying a Swede or English or whatever he is. He's a stranger. You should marry a Croat. Your brother is marrying Emmeline. She's one of our people."

"Matt loves Emmeline, Mama," said Mary. "He isn't engaged to her because of her background. He loves her because she's a swell gal."

"She's one of us," said Ma.

"Mama, Roger Thompson is an American," Mary pleaded. "He's one of us!" She sounded on the verge of tears. "That's what we are now, not Croats or Lithuanians or Swedes."

"You are forgetting your roots," said Ma, her voice low and harsh.

"Give him a chance," said Mary. "Please."

"He never asked my permission to court you," said Ma. "He never asked Yosip's permission. It's indecent."

"This is America, Mama. This is 1925. A girl gets to pick her own husband now. If he proposes, I'll say yes whether you like it or not. At least he's not a drinker, like Papa was." I heard the clear, hard smack of Ma's hand across my sister's face. Thompson droned on in the sitting room.

An owl called out above the cow barn. I heard the kitchen door swing open.

Ma spoke her first English words of the night. "Boys, take the Mr. Roger for a sodypop, eh?" she called out. "Mary, she is sick."

"Why, that's too bad," said Thompson. "I hope she gets well real soon." I heard chairs being pushed back from the table. I folded up the newspaper and shoved it into my back pocket. I opened the door wide enough to look in. I could see past Ma into the sitting room. "But I'd enjoy a bottle of soda or two with the boys. Thanks for the supper, Mrs. Petrovich. Tell Mary I'll see her around."

Ma nodded and turned away. Her face was the color of ashes and her eyes shone bright and black like new coal.

We all knew that look. It meant that Ma was a whole lot more than mad. I thanked my lucky stars that I wasn't in Mary's shoes. Just then Philip came running up. "I forgot my pocketknife," he said.

"Don't go in," I said. "Too dangerous."

"Is it because of the Swede?" asked Philip.

"He's not a Swede," I said.

"He looks like one," said Philip. "Girls are such knuckleheads. Mary'll go to hell if she marries a Lutheran."

"What do you need a knife for?" I asked.

"Mumblety-peg," said Philip. "Can I borrow yours? Pinky said he'll give me one of his ducklings if I beat him."

"What if you lose?"

"I have to clean their hog pen for a week," said Philip. "But I like pigs, so it's worth it." I dug my knife out of my pocket and handed it to Philip.

"I'll slice off your nose if you lose it," I said. Philip's hand flew to his face. Matt had given me the knife for memorizing the times tables all the way to the twenties when I was Philip's age. It was twice the size of most boys' pocketknives and had three blades instead of only one.

"I swear I won't lose it," said Philip. "And if I win, I'll let you name the duckling."

"Sharpen it before you bring it back," I said, but Philip was already halfway across the yard.

I wandered down to the barn, stopping at the trough to pump myself a drink of water. Daisy was still in her stanchion, munching on hay. I climbed up and draped myself over her warm, fat back.

The town clock struck nine. In three hours Perks and Skinny would be waiting for me down at the grape train. Daisy shifted her weight and flicked me with her long tail. Mary was loony to think Ma would let her hitch up with a fellow who wasn't bohunk like us. Would Mary elope? Ma would never forgive her for that. And what did my brothers know about this Thompson fellow? Why had they been so quiet? Usually they were jolly with company, at least Matt always was, and Joey was friendly even if he was quiet. Something was up, and I didn't like being in the dark.

I yanked my thoughts back to the grape train. Tons and tons of grapes were waiting to be swiped, no matter who Mary wanted to marry. I grinned and scratched Daisy on the shoulder. My pals were depending on me. I wouldn't let them down.

I thought through the details one by one. The plan would work. In a few short hours my pals and I would be stuffing our faces after pulling off the grape heist of the century.

I climbed down and found a pile of clean hay near the window. I unfolded the *Miner's Echo* and read until it was too dark to see.

Chapter Five

The town clock chimed eleven-forty-five and my heart started to thump loud enough to wake the dead. I rolled out of bed without a sound. Philip didn't move a muscle. So far so good.

The attic windows were open at each end and the moon lit up the whole place. Joey and Matt's bed was empty. It seemed likely to me that the big boys and Mr. Thompson had found something more entertaining than sodypop to drink.

I picked my overalls up off the floor and tiptoed across the room. I climbed down the ladder, listened to make sure Ma and Mary were sleeping, then pussyfooted it across the kitchen. I pulled on my overalls and sneaked past the cookstove and out the back door. I could hear shouting down at the Brick Saloon. The miners were snockered, like always.

I hurried down the hill. When I passed the Brick I peeked in. Two guys were scuffling, and it looked like it might turn out to be a good one. I fought the urge to stay and watch. The grapes and my pals were waiting.

The train was out back on the stretch of track behind Marko's Grocery. The boxcars looked huge in the moonlight, and so did the railroad bull with his nightstick. It was Big Swede, six foot eight and mean as a bobcat with one foot caught in a trap.

Perks grabbed my arm and pulled me behind some empty crates. Skinny was squatting on the ground, breathing hard. "I got here early and been watching things," said Perks. Even though there was plenty of background noise from the nearly two dozen soda joints and their late-night patrons, we whispered anyhow. "Ma let me off early on account of bellyache."

"So what's the lay of the land?" I asked.

"Big Swede's got a snootful," said Perks. "I seen him step into Slim's and come out with a bottle, and it wasn't Schwab's Sodypop, neither."

"Pop said folks already bought a few boxes of grapes, right after the train pulled in," said Skinny. "But mostly the cars are full."

"Perks, Big Swede is all yours," I whispered. Perks grinned and saluted. "This year I'm going for three boxes. You're gonna have to catch each one, Skinny, and don't let any fall to the ground. Got it?" Skinny nodded. "Soon as we've snagged the goods we meet behind the Brick Saloon," I said.

"You positive this'll work?" asked Skinny.

"You chicken?" I asked. He shook his head. "Don't forget, I got the secret weapon." I patted my overalls pocket. Skinny grinned.

Perks elbowed me and pointed with his thumb in the direction of the boxcars. The three of us crouched even lower. Big Swede passed ten feet in front of our hiding spot. Even from that distance I could smell hooch. Big Swede was crocked.

I rubbed my hands together. A chill ran up my back, and my arms went chicken-skinned. If we pulled it off, we'd soon be gorging ourselves on Black Bear wine grapes, all the way from California.

Big Swede passed behind the boxcars.

"Remember what I told you. Now—go!" I said. Perks jumped up and headed toward the caboose end of the train. I could smell Skinny's sweat. I dug my toes into the gravel under my feet and was glad I didn't wear boots in the summer the way Skinny did.

Perks hollered in the darkness. "Hey, Mr. Northern Pacific Railroad bull man!"

"Who's dere?" came the reply.

"I seen the bottle!" yelled Perks. "Ain't that *moon-shine*, Big Swede? I'm gonna tell your boss you been drinking on the night watch. Or maybe I'll tell the feds. Maybe you Swedes is too stupid to know moon-shine ain't legal. You big *klantskalle!*" I bit my lip to keep from laughing. Perks had just called Big Swede a blockhead. Skinny clapped a chubby hand over his mouth.

"You kid, you get outta here!" hollered the bull in a singsong Swedish accent. "Shut your mouth and go home or I call the sheriff."

"Hee-hee!" Perks giggled. "Hey, *ditt svin,* you're too stewed to take a step. You're so pig-eyed you can't see to pee. *Dumhuvud!*"

Skinny doubled over laughing. Big Swede swore and I heard his footsteps as he started to run toward Perks's voice.

"Help!" yelled Perks. "The big ol' Northern Pacific *tjockskalle* gonna kill the skinny little colored boy." You swine. Dumb cluck. Fathead. I'd learned a dozen insults in Swede from Big Swede's kid Lenny and taught them to Perks. I'd made him practice until he got the pronunciation just right. Now all the hard work was paying off. Big Swede was nowhere in sight. I elbowed Skinny and we took off toward the boxcars.

"Keep those boots quiet!" I whispered to Skinny.

"Mama!" screamed Perks from way down the train tracks. Skinny stopped.

"Do you think he's hurt?" he asked.

"Nah, he's faking," I said, pulling on Skinny and hoping to high heaven that I was right.

When we got to the train, I looked around first for competition. If there were other boys out there, I couldn't see or hear any. I chose a boxcar.

"That one," I said to Skinny. It was mostly in shadow, the last one in the line.

Skinny gave me a leg up to the first rung of the boxcar ladder. While I climbed to the top, he pulled back the lower bolt, but that wasn't enough to open the door. The railroad had gotten wise to us. For the last couple of years they'd locked the boxcar doors at the top. I lay flat on the top of the car and slid myself over to where the upper bolt was locked shut. I felt for the big padlock. When I had it in my hand, I grinned.

Last year, after the grape train had left town, I'd wandered around behind Marko's looking for any stray grapes on the ground. I didn't find grapes. I found a broken lock, one of the big ones the railroad used to keep out us boys. Someone, maybe even my cousins, had broken the lock clean off. I took the lock home, fixed it, and learned how to pick it open.

I'd practiced all year with picks I'd made out of nails. Perks was screaming in the distance, and Skinny was sweating down below. It was all up to me.

I leaned over and stuck one of the nails into the hole. I jiggled it around until I heard a click. Then I pulled out the nail and stuck in a second one. I felt the inside of the lock just the way I'd done a hundred times before. I pulled down, shoved the nail in at an angle, pushed and wiggled it, and then the lock fell open.

"Got it!" I whispered down to Skinny. He pulled the big sliding door open, and the smell of grapes seemed to pour into the night air. I figured the whole state of California must smell this sweet.

Perks screeched in the dark and then he laughed. So far so good. I climbed down the ladder and crawled in onto the top of the stack of boxes. I lay on my belly and whispered down to Skinny, "You ready?"

"Yeah. Throw 'em down nice and easy, one at a time," he said, and then he crossed himself like any good Catholic boy about to steal sixty pounds of grapes. I wiggled the first crate over toward the side.

"Look out below!" I said, and dropped the box. I heard a thud. The next thing I knew, Skinny was flat on his back and the grapes were all over the ground.

Chapter Six

I scrambled down the ladder and jumped to the ground. Skinny was out cold. I smacked his cheeks. "Skinny," I whispered. "Wake up!" I shook him. I snapped the top of his head. Finally he groaned.

"*Gesù!*" he said. His hand went to his forehead, where even in the moonlight I could see a lump swelling up. "Did I catch 'em, Cuss?"

"No, you fat wop," I said. "The grapes are all over the ground. We gotta get outta here. Big Swede'll be back in no time." I looked down the tracks in the direction Perks had run, hoping my little pal was OK. Skinny sat up.

"The grapes!" he said. We heard Big Swede's voice in the distance.

"Forget it," I said, feeling sick to my stomach from the thought of hightailing it without our grapes. We might as well have been walking away from Blackbeard's treasure.

"No!" cried Skinny. He stood up, staggered a step, then started picking up bunches of grapes and tossing them back into the crate. "I don't want to wait a whole year for another chance."

I picked up a bunch. It was heavy with tight, ripe grapes. They were as black as coal in the moonlight. In half a minute the box was full. I picked it up. One box was better than nothing.

"You boys, stop dere!" yelled Big Swede. He was heading toward us, swaying from side to side as he tried to hurry.

"Skinny!" I yelled. "Make tracks!" We ran around Marko's Grocery and across the street. The box of grapes was heavy, but it didn't slow me down. Skinny huffed and puffed, holding his head but keeping up with me. We circled down around Mount Pisgah Presbyterian Church and stopped to catch our breath. Big Swede was nowhere in sight.

"We gave him the slip," said Skinny, gasping for air between each word.

"He can't wander off from the train. We ain't the only boys who'll be after those grapes tonight," I said, thinking about my cousins Turk and Putzy, who'd bragged that this year they'd steal a hundred pounds of grapes with their hands tied behind their backs. Big Swede was in for a busy night.

Skinny grabbed a handful of grapes and shoved them into his mouth. Juice squirted out and dribbled around his lips.

"Quit stuffing your face and let's go find Perks," I said, hoping like anything that he'd gotten away from Big Swede. Boys who'd gotten caught in the past couldn't sit down for a week.

"I can't run anymore," said Skinny. "How 'bout I stay here and protect the goods and you go get him?"

"An' leave 'em unprotected from you?" I said.

"I won't touch another one," said Skinny through the mouthful. "I swear." He crossed himself to show his sincerity. If Skinny swore, he meant it.

"I'll get him and come right back." I started for the Brick Saloon, two blocks away.

Perks was right where we'd planned, behind the saloon's outhouse. "Did you get 'em?" he asked.

"Only one box. Skinny's guarding it over behind Mount Pisgah."

"I thought you had a brain, Cuss," said Perks. "Don't you know Skinny'll eat 'em in three gulps if we ain't there to stop him? We better hurry. I didn't take no size number twelve boot in my butt for noth-ing. I want my share."

"Big Swede got you?" I asked.

"Right in the hinder," said Perks. "Twice." He rubbed his behind. "I tripped over a tie and he caught up, loaded and swearin' in Swede." Perks chuckled. "Guess I got all the words right."

"Nice job," I said, pulling on his arm. "Let's skedaddle." We started back toward the church, and I told Perks about dropping the box and how Skinny was out cold for a few seconds. He laughed so loud I had to tell him to shut up. We kept off the main street and made our way behind stores and down the alley.

We were half a block from the church when I heard my brother Matt's voice coming from the shad-ows between two store buildings. Matt had gotten away with more than a few grapes in his day.

"Go on and find Skinny," I said to Perks. "I'll catch up in a jiff." Perks loped off in the direction of Skinny's hiding place, and I went to find my brother. I knew he'd get a chuckle hearing about our adven-ture. Maybe he'd even want to join us for a few ripe ones.

I turned into an alley and stopped short. Joey was fifteen feet away standing behind Roger Thompson, holding him by the arms. I could smell liquor from where I stood. Matt stood in front of Thompson, his hands made into fists.

"You're crazy," said Thompson, his words slurred from booze. So much for him not being a drinker. "Let me go."

"It's him," said Joey. "I'm sure." Matt pulled back and slammed his fist into Thompson's face. Thompson groaned as the blood poured from his nose. I felt sour bile rise up into my throat. I choked it back down.

"Stay away from our sister," said Matt. "Got it?"

I took a step backward. I felt like heaving. I'd never once heard Matt holler in anger, let alone hit anyone. I wanted to run away, but I couldn't drag myself from what I'd seen.

"You'd better get out of town," said Matt. "We know what you're up to. We know your real name."

"Ronald Simms," said Joey.

"Let me go," said Thompson. His lower face was covered in blood.

"Joey was at the livestock auction in Yakima last month," said Matt. "He saw the Wanted poster in the Western Union office, didn't you, Joe?" Matt's voice was tight and high with rage. It didn't even sound like him.

"Blond fellow," said Joey. "Ladies' man. Alias Thompson, Tomkins, Thomas. Wanted for murder."

"The feds are after you," said Matt.

"Mind your own business, scum boys," said Thompson. But that wasn't his name, was it? He spit on the ground next to Matt's feet.

"Get out," said Matt. "I don't want to see your face in this town again." He nodded at Joey to release Simms, a wanted man who had been in our house making sweet to Mary. Simms staggered and wiped his face on his sleeve.

"You'll pay for this." His voice was drunk and full of spite. "I have friends in Seattle, Spokane, Portland — you name it. You're nothing. This trash-heap town is nothing." He turned around and spit again at my brothers. "Foreigner swine."

Joey lunged toward Simms but Matt grabbed him and held him back. Simms dodged and staggered backward. He caught his foot in an empty wooden box next to the wall and lost his footing. His arms flew back. He tried to catch himself, but his foot was stuck and there was nothing but air to grab. I heard the thud of his head as it hit the brick wall. I heard a dull snap, like a stick of kindling wrapped in a rag, and I heard his breath go out of him in a whoosh, and then the soft brush of his clothes against the brick as he slid to the ground and was still.

I didn't breathe until Joey prodded Simms with one foot. He bent over, poked around, then stood up.

"Neck's snapped," he said. I sucked in my breath. Matt and Joey jerked their heads and saw me for the first time. Matt swore.

I was shaking all over and whimpering like a puppy.

"Quiet," said Joey. I nodded and held my breath again.

"Me and Joey got everything under control, Cuss," said Matt. "You just keep quiet about all of this." I nodded again and crossed myself, swearing a silent oath. "Now get home, little brother. Double time."

I turned and ran.

Chapter Seven

When I got home I tiptoed into the house, went upstairs, and lay down on the bed without bothering to take off my overalls. The night was hot but I shivered like I had the influenza. The clock struck one, then two. The saloons closed down and the town turned quiet. I heard an owl. I heard our rooster. I listened to my own breathing. I counted the times Philip turned over. The clock struck three. The back door opened. I heard whispers and then low voices and the click of the electric lightbulb being switched on in the kitchen.

Ma called out quietly, "Mary, get up." Then there was some talk in Croatian, but I couldn't hear what they said. Half of me wanted to creep across the room, point my ear downstairs, and listen. The other half wanted to bury my head under the quilt and hum "Yankee Doodle Dandy" to drown out the awful thoughts that felt like they might turn my guts to water.

When the sun came up, I woke Philip and we went down to breakfast. Matt and Joey were at the table drinking coffee. Ma said Mary was in bed with a sick headache, so for the second time in a row I milked my cow and hers both. Philip showed me the duckling he'd won in the game. He said I could name it, but I told him to do it himself, that I couldn't think of anything.

Would the sheriff come for Matt and Joey? All during breakfast, Philip yammered on and on about the duck. No one else said a word. Breakfast did not sit well in my belly.

Matt and Joey went off to work, just like they did every day. Ma was grim.

After the boys left, I drove the cows up into the hills and left them to graze for the day. When I got home I helped Philip clean the pigpen. His sick piglet had died in the night, and his lower lip trembled the whole time he talked about it. I patted his head and told him there'd be other piglets, but I was only listening with half an ear.

After we cleaned out the pigpen, Ma told us to dig

a new trench for the outhouse and move it. It'd been two years since we'd had a new trench, and you could tell by the smell that it was time. Philip groaned, swore, and spit. I got the pickax and Philip got the shovel. We marked a spot three big paces away from the outhouse, then started to dig, piling the fresh dirt onto a canvas tarpaulin. By lunchtime the hole was as deep as I was tall.

Digging hard helped me not to think too much, but no matter how I sweated and pounded the ground with the pickax, I couldn't forget what I'd seen.

Perks and Skinny showed up that afternoon, brimming over with the big news that a dead man had been found behind the bakery. They also wanted to know why I hadn't come back for my share of the grapes.

"You went after grapes again?" Philip asked. "How come you never bring me?"

"It's dangerous business, that's why," said Perks. "Check out the egg on Skinny's head." Skinny lifted his cap so we could all see the lump.

I told the boys that I'd puked all night and wasn't up to eating grapes, and for them to go ahead and eat the rest. They were none too unhappy about that, but what they really wanted to yak about was the dead man.

He'd been found dead around five-thirty A.M. by Sparky Stepanovich, a kid Philip's age who worked picking rocks out of the coal at the Number Three.

"Pop says it's murder," said Skinny. "The guy was all bloody."

I swallowed the lump in my throat and pitched a shovelful of dirt onto the pile.

"No," said Perks, "it ain't murder, it's an accident. Granny talked to the undertaker's wife and she said the guy's neck was snapped clean and the back of his head was bruised. Her husband could see plain as your nose that the guy was drunk and fell."

"Pop said the dead man's name is Thompson," said Skinny.

Philip stopped digging. His face was pale. "Thompson?" he said. "Mary's friend?"

I broke up the ground with the pickax. My arms ached and the dirt flew. Sweat trickled into my eyes.

"One of Pop's customers told him it looked like a hit," said Skinny.

"You don't know squat, Skinny," said Perks. I looked up at my pals. They were staring down at me. "It was an accident," said Perks. "Everyone knows it."

"He was just at our house last night," said Philip. "Mary invited him for—"

"Shut up, Philip," I said, and pointed the pickax toward the outhouse. "You and me got work to do."

For a minute no one said anything. Then Perks and Skinny said they had to go. I didn't look up.

Philip and I dragged the outhouse to the new hole and filled in the old hole with the fresh dirt, tamping it down with our feet once it was safe to step on.

That day, five of my six aunts on Ma's side stopped by. I didn't have to be there to know what they had come to talk about.

"Aunt Katja said 'Thompson' wasn't that guy's name," said Philip after I sent him to fetch the bucket of whitewash for the inside of the outhouse. "And he was a criminal," said Philip. "A gangster. Do you think he had a tommy gun?"

"Gimme the brush," I said. I painted the ceiling and sides where Philip couldn't reach, then handed him back the brush. My head was pounding from the heat and the work and the smell of the outhouse and my own sweat. I leaned against the outside of the outhouse and took a breather.

"Do you think he was a mobster?" asked Philip. "Do you think Mary knew he was a mobster?"

"Of course not," I snapped. "Enough already about the dead guy." I flicked a fly off my shoulder and slid down to the ground, tired all the way to the bone. Philip whitewashed without talking. I could hear the aunts inside the house.

"I wish we had a flushing crapper like Uncle Tony's," said Philip.

"Uncle Tony's rich," I said, "on account of making slivovitz."

"Cuss, is Uncle Tony a bootlegger?" asked Philip.

"Of course not," I said, but I wasn't so sure. Making and selling booze were illegal. Uncle Tony cooked up his Old Country plum brew and sold it to the ethnics for funerals and weddings. I'd never thought of him as a bootlegger, but maybe he was. I didn't want to talk about it.

"You know why we won't ever get a flushing crapper?" I asked. Philip shook his head. "Because if we did, you'd sit there all day pullin' the chain."

"Says you," said Philip, and he showed off the gap in his teeth with a big smile.

I dipped my finger into the whitewash and flicked it at Philip's head.

"Hey!" he hollered, but he was too slow. I slammed the outhouse door shut before he could get his revenge and ran to the wash house. I pumped the water until it ran ice cold. Then I stuck my head under the stream until I was half drowned. It took my breath away, but it didn't wash the thoughts out of my skull.

Mr. Giombetti's customer had said it looked like a hit. If folks knew Matt and Joey had been with the dead man, did they think my brothers were mixed up in the bootlegging business? That they were somehow connected to mobsters?

I knew the truth. I'd seen it, all of it, and I couldn't say a word. I'd seen the whole thing, but who would believe me?

When Joey and Matt didn't come home after work that night, I knew the rumors were only going to get worse.

Chapter Eight

Ma was all smiles at suppertime.

"A man was in town recruiting workers for a lumber camp over west of the mountains," she said in Croatian. "He offered Yosip and Mate nine dollars a day each, and they went with him."

"Nine?" cried Philip. "Hell's bells!"

"The work starts tomorrow," said Ma. "Isn't that wonderful? Praised be Jesus and Mary." Ma spooned big globs of beet greens and brown gravy onto our plates. She passed around fried ham and a bowl of boiled potatoes.

"They'll be rich," said Philip, his eyes wide as saucers. "I've never even seen nine bucks."

"What about Emmeline?" I asked in Croatian. Matt was supposed to be getting married soon. He had it bad for Emmeline, and it was no wonder. She was a little thing, bright and full of smiles. Matt always called her "Missy Itty Bitty."

"Mate will work it out," said Ma. She talked about how lucky my brothers were to get those new jobs. She didn't say a word about the dead man. Mary was still sick in her room.

I was on my way out to feed scraps to the chickens when Ma handed me an envelope with my name written on it. "Mate told me to give this to you," she said. "Before he left."

"*Hvala,*" I said. *Thanks.* As soon as I was in the barn, I opened the envelope. Inside was a letter to me, a silver dollar, and another envelope sealed shut with the name "Emmeline" written on the front. I tilted my letter toward the open barn door so I could see it better. This is what it said:

Salutations, Cuss,

When Lady Luck calls, a feller has to answer, so here I go off to the wild woods to swing the ax and fell the mighty forest. How's that for Manifest Destiny? A big adventure, and this lad is up for it. Ha-ha! I can already smell the moolah. Nice thing about lumberjacking is, you don't have to crouch. No more aching back, no more digging in the deep black hole.

About a certain scuffle—let's keep that between you and me. Don't worry your head, little brother, and don't talk to strangers. Leave everything to me and Joe. Keep up with the school business, OK?

Us lumberjacks are always a-moving, so heaven knows when I'll see you again. Just wanted to say so long, and take care of Ma and the rest while I'm off making my pot of gold.

Cuss, I'm hiring you to do a job because you're the man of the house now, so listen up. Take this other note to Emmeline. You know how girls worry when their Prince Charming is out of sight. Here's a buck for your trouble. Buy yourself a book or something.

Your Gypsy brother, Matt

I stared at the letter and the money. I'd never had a silver dollar in my life. I'd never had a letter either. Why'd Matt and Joey run off like they did? If it was just an accident, if everyone knew Simms was a crook on the lam, why the quick exit? Why not stick around and tell the truth? Couldn't the lumberjack jobs wait until they were in the clear? I'd back them up. I'd seen the whole thing. Wasn't the law on the side of the truth?

I felt danger hanging in the air like a fog. Ma was worried. She'd acted cheerful about my brothers getting new jobs, and I'd never known her to tell a lie, but still, the look on her face when she'd talked about Matt and Joey and the lumber camp recruiter left me scratching my head.

The town was talking. No one said it to my face but I knew the gist. My brothers had run from the law. They'd acted like rabbits instead of heroes. It didn't make sense.

I folded the letter back up and stuck it in my pocket with the dollar. I finished my chores and told Ma I'd be gone for a minute. I ran down the hill and across the neighborhood to the Cimmermanceks' house. Emmeline's older brother, Inky, answered the door.

"Hey, Cuss," he said. His black eyes stared into mine. Inky'd quit school at eleven and was beating up full-grown men by the time he was thirteen. His fists and his drinking were famous.

"Got something for your sister," I said.

"Which one?" said Inky. "There's six of 'em."

"Emmeline," I said. Inky shut the door in my face and I waited there, hoping I wouldn't have to stand around for too long. It seemed odd to me that a gal as sweet as Emmeline could have a brother as bad as Inky.

But I never saw Emmeline. Instead, her mother showed up at the door looking grim. I said hello and that I had a letter for Emmeline. She nodded, took the letter, and thanked me. Then she closed the door.

Did Mrs. Cimmermancek think Matt and Joey had killed that crook? That they were murderers? My heart fell down to my gut with a thud. What mother would let her daughter read a letter from a murderer?

I'd let Matt down. He'd asked me to give the letter to Emmeline. I'd given it to her ma instead.

When I got home, I showed the silver dollar to Philip.

"This is for you, from Matt," I lied. Philip did an Indian dance in a circle until he was dizzy and fell in a heap on the ground. I hefted the weight of the shiny dollar once and tossed it down to him. "Don't spend it all in one place," I said. I'd fouled up the one important thing my brother had asked me to do. What a heel. I couldn't keep his money.

Over the next few days neighbors and relatives dropped by to see Ma. In town I ran into kids from school. Everyone had questions. We told the same story again and again. Joey and Matt had gone west of the mountains to cut timber. We'd be hearing from them any day now. They were earning nine bucks a day cutting trees. Yes, Simms had eaten at our house, but that was all we knew. Ma didn't like him. Her bad elbow started to throb the minute he stepped onto the porch. Mary wasn't mixed up with any crook. That was just nasty gossip. It was the boys who'd invited Simms for dinner. As for Mary, didn't they know that Clement Bovitz had been sweet on her for years?

Chapter Nine

On Monday Perks and I hunted for blackberries while the cows nibbled grass on the hills. Out of the blue Perks said, "There's talk, Cuss."

"So?" I said. Of course there was talk.

"The sheriff is in the know."

"About what? The grapes? Guess you and Skinny'll have to puke them up for evidence." I forced out a chuckle.

"You dunce. I mean the connection—between the dead man and your brothers."

"There's no connection at all, and anyone who says so is a lying dog," I said.

"Yeah, well, says you, but I hear things," he said, "as in your brothers went to the sheriff, told him the whole thing, and he told 'em to get outta town for fear of the mobsters."

"My brothers got new jobs," I said, hiding the surprise I felt. What did bootleggers have to do with Matt and Joey? And how come I hadn't heard anything about them going to the sheriff? "They're getting nine bucks a day cutting trees. They didn't run away from anything."

"My uncle Willie's a lumberjack over in Enumclaw," said Perks. "He don't make no nine bucks."

"Then he works for a cheap outfit."

"Cuss, I'm saying they was smart to get away," said Perks. "There's talk that two out-of-town boys was sniffin' around Roslyn last Friday, asking questions afterward, you know. Some say they're mobsters, itchin' to get revenge on account of that dead man was one of their boys. So see, I know why your brothers left. I know the whole thing, and I'm your best pal, so you can tell me where they are. I keep a secret. I'm the same as a bird. I drink water but I don't pee."

"They're west of the mountains. Matt wrote me a letter." I tossed a rock at a pine stump. It bounced off with a thud. Could mobsters really be after my brothers? "When the work runs out there, they'll be back."

I'd thought my brothers had run off from the law.

This news was worse. I felt the hairs on the back of my neck stand up, and my mouth went dry.

"There's more—I mean, if you want to hear," said Perks. "But maybe you don't think I know diddly-squat." I shrugged and stooped to pick up more rocks. "All of us sodypop joints, we all got our own supply of 'shine," he said.

"That ain't news," I said. I threw a rock at the stump and missed.

"It works out," said Perks, "on account of every-one keeping to his own supplier. Nobody gets greedy, everybody gets by, and the business stays right here in Roslyn. Coloreds buy from colored bootleggers in town, white folks buy from white bootleggers in town. There's no hits at all, and everybody gets along. So far. But there's talk of trouble.

"See, the city boys, the big-time mobsters, they want all the business in the whole country. They want to make and sell all the booze. They don't want there to be no little independent bootleggers."

I hit the stump. Perks kept talking.

"There's twenty-two drink joints in Roslyn, and that's the ones with a front door. So the mobsters from the city say to themselves, 'Hey, let's us get a piece o' that,' and they send out a chump like Simms to make deals, to get all the drink joints to start buying from his mob, and if they don't make a deal, they get leaned on.

"That boy Simms was sent by the Mob to deal, and nobody was dealin', so he was starting to lean," said Perks.

I hit the stump twice in a row. It burned my guts to think of that lousy crook making sweet to my sister. Matt was right to flatten his face. "You're saying Joey and Matt knew all this?"

"They only knew he was a wanted man. The sheriff filled them in later. That Simms killed a U.S. marshal in Wyoming. Knifed him."

"Matt and Joey didn't kill Simms." I stopped myself from saying that I'd been there, that I'd seen the whole thing, that I knew exactly how he'd died.

"The whole town knows they didn't do it," said Perks. "They was smart to hightail it. 'Fact, sheriff told 'em to get out."

"Joey and Matt are cutting trees," I said, forcing my voice to sound bored with all the talk. "That's all I know for sure."

"I hope that lumber camp is someplace far away from here, like Texas."

That night there was a big fight at Slim's. Johnny Kotula and Ham Plesha had a go. It all started when Kotula let out a string of curses, pulled a knife, and slashed Ham across one arm. Ham hauled off and hit Kotula, who went down for the count. The other guys tried to wake Kotula with a bucket of beer in the face, but it didn't do any good. He never did wake up. Two days later he croaked.

The next day a gang of Kotula's pals beat Ham to a bloody pulp.

Over the next couple of weeks the rumors went around and around in Roslyn like buzzards over a dead dog. Ham and Kotula were local bootleggers. There was talk of double-crossing and stolen profits. Some said Kotula had made a deal with some big-city mobsters. As the days went by, the stories got worse. Folks stopped talking about my brothers, but I didn't stop worrying.

One night Philip was still awake when I got into bed. "You should sleep in Joey and Matt's bed," he said.

"And where will they sleep when they come back?"

Philip didn't answer.

I climbed into bed beside him and lay awake for a long time. School was only two weeks away. I tried to cheer myself up thinking about it, but it didn't do much good.

I had a hundred and one questions and no answers.

Chapter Ten

On the first day of school I got up at four, did my chores, ate breakfast, and delivered milk, cream, and butter to Ma's customers. I washed my face and put on a new pair of socks Ma had knitted, and Matt's old boots with a page of the *Miner's Echo* stuffed in the toes. After all those months with nothing on my feet, socks and boots would take some getting used to. Ma gave me and Philip a penny each to pay for our pencils. Philip headed to Pinky's house. I ran down the hill to Giombetti's Butcher Shop.

I met up with Skinny, who was coming out the front door. His shoes were brand-new, ordered from Sears Roebuck. He grinned and adjusted his cap. The cap was new, too.

By the time we got to the schoolhouse, I'd wiped all the eagerness off my mug. A guy who liked school too much was liable to get pounded.

Miss Henley was the new seventh-grade teacher. She had black hair with a white stripe on one side, so right off we called her "Skunky" behind her back. She called roll, starting at the beginning of the alphabet. Perks sat at the desk in front of me. "Percival Lincoln Perkins?" said Skunky.

"Here," said Perks.

"Slava Petrovich?"

"Here," I said. She continued on down the list—Lips Rickman, Mabel Suivonen—until she ended up with Koha Zdon. There were forty-three of us that morning, down nine from last year on account of all the boys who had quit school last June to work in the mines.

I felt so fine sitting there at my desk that I could almost forget my brothers were gone and there was trouble in our town. We got our arithmetic books and a book of short stories. I read a quick one about a tiger hunt while Skunky went over the class rules. Later Skunky passed out brand-new grammar books. I wrote my name on the inside cover—Slava J. Petrovich—and then I thumbed through the book and read about diagramming sentences. The bell rang and we filed out to recess.

There were fights at lunchtime. Biscuit Mara ended up with a broken arm and Fishface Flannery got expelled, so by one that afternoon our class was down to forty-one.

After lunch Skunky told us to take out a piece of paper. "Listen carefully as I read this poem aloud. Then write two paragraphs in your best penmanship about what you think it means."

She opened a book and read "When I Heard the Learned Astronomer" by Walt Whitman.

"When I heard the learned astronomer,
When the proofs, the figures, were ranged in
    columns before me,
When I was shown the charts and diagrams, to
    add, divide, and measure them,
When I sitting heard the astronomer where he
    lectured with much applause in the lecture
    room,
How soon unaccountable I became tired and sick
Till rising and gliding out I wandered off by myself,
In the mystical moist night-air, and from time to
    time,
Looked up in perfect silence at the stars."

Skunky closed the book. "Please begin writing," she said.

My brothers were hiding from mobsters and my boots didn't fit, but just then I let everything else sit on the back bench of my brain. Every summer I forgot how much I loved school. Every September I remembered.

I scratched out an essay. The paper was smooth and clean, and my pencil was as sharp as a pin. I wrote that a fellow can like looking at stars without knowing much about them. I wrote that the astronomer was very interested in star science and maybe sometimes that made him forget that stars were worth looking at even if you didn't know squat about what made them twinkle. I finished by writing that even so, if I had the chance, I'd go to hear the learned astronomer myself, and after that, the stars would never look the same again.

By the end of the first week of school, eight more boys had dropped out to work. The mines were short of workers, and twelve or thirteen years old was close enough, even if it wasn't legal.

The next Monday Ma sent all the milk with me to sell and didn't keep back any for our family. "The weather is too hot," she said. "I don't want it to go bad. Might as well sell it."

That night at suppertime, Philip piped up. "Do you think I could work picking coal instead of going to school? Pinky says they pay a dime a day. He said I could pass for ten, easy. Then I could buy some pigs of my own. I hate school. I'm not like Cuss." He pointed at the book of short stories. It was on the table next to my plate.

"Pinky has feathers in his head," said Ma in Croatian. "You are only seven. Stay in school for now, my little one."

"But, Mama, I want to earn some money," said Philip in English.

"Joey and Matt will send money," said Ma, switching to English. "From cutting trees. You be a schoolboy—you and Slava."

"We won't have Mary's wages after she's hitched," said Philip, pointing his fork in Mary's direction.

"What?" I asked, and just about dropped my knife. "Not Hairy?"

Mary elbowed me in the gut. "Who else?" she said. Her face was the color of beets. She spread the food around on her plate but didn't take a bite or look up. "He's come calling twice a week for the last month, but you're always too busy fooling around with your friends or sitting with your nose stuck in the newspaper to notice."

"I listened through the floorboards when he proposed last night," said Philip, grinning like a demon.

Mary smiled and we all laughed.

"Cuss could work, Mama," said Mary, "if you need him to. Look how big he's getting."

"Slava stays in school," said Ma. "I have decided." I breathed a silent sigh of relief. Matt and Joey went to work when they were my age. Neither of them went to the seventh grade.

Ma said Joey and Matt would send money. When they did, we wouldn't miss Mary's wages at all. No one else would have to work.

Someone knocked at the door. It was Hairy Bovitz, asking if Mary could go for a stroll. I wondered what had changed Mary's mind about the guy, but I decided not to ask. No use getting her riled up at me.

After evening chores I sat out on the front porch to read short stories. I was about halfway through one about a king from a place called Aquitaine when I looked up and saw Emmeline and her mother walking up the hill. I thought about the letter I'd handed over to her mother and felt like a heel all over again. I felt my ears turn red. I tried to concentrate on the story, hoping Emmeline and her ma would pass right by, but when Emmeline said, "Hi, Cuss," I had to look up. She smiled and winked and I knew right then and there that she'd gotten the letter. I grinned like an idiot.

Emmeline's hair was jet-black, and she had light hazel-colored eyes that turned up at the corners. Matt said they were Old Country eyes. With one pretty look Emmeline had lifted a load off my back. I could have hugged her, even if she was a girl.

I stuck my head inside the house and hollered for Ma. She came out to the porch with a dish towel in her hand, ready to give me a snap on the behind for hollering at her. But when Ma saw Emmeline and Mrs. Cimmermancek, she smiled and broke into loud, happy Croatian chitchat.

The two older women hugged and blabbed. First they asked about each other's relatives and whether anyone had heard anything from anyone in the Old Country. Then they talked about the new electric clothes iron for sale in the general store ("Who needs an electric? They don't get as hot as ones you heat on the stove"), Ma's apple trees ("Loaded this year"), Mrs. Fiori's twins ("The one died, but thank God it was baptized in the nick of time"), the high price of coffee ("God help us, seven cents a pound"), and the trouble with boys ("They eat like an army, grow too fast, and don't stay clean").

While they were talking, Hairy brought Mary home. She joined in the chatter. I decided to make myself scarce and was just about to find a quiet spot where I could finish my reading when I saw Emmeline draw a folded piece of paper out of her dress pocket and hand it to her mother.

"We have news," said Mrs. Cimmermancek, low-ering her voice to a near whisper. She was still speak-ing Croatian, and she looked over at me to see if I understood.

I put on a dumb look and stared at a sentence describing the king's favorite falcon. My ears were tuned to pick up the smallest speck of information.

Ma was not fooled by the dumb look. "Slava, feed the cows," she said. The three women went inside and I moseyed over to the barn in a funk. Something was up, and I would have bet a dollar it was about Matt and Joey.

Philip came out to feed the pigs.

"Did you hear anything?" I asked.

"No, they talked in whispers, in Croatian." Philip's Croatian wasn't the best. He had a hard time keeping up if folks talked fast. He wiped his nose on his sleeve. "Matt sent a letter," he said. "And money. That's all I heard. I already gave Ma my silver dollar. I was gonna buy some more ducks, but I could tell she was worried. She quit putting sugar in the coffee."

I mussed up my little brother's hair and yanked his ear. "It ain't your job to support the family, squirt," I said. "You leave that to the big boys."

"Are you gonna quit school?" asked Philip.

I flicked a spider off the fence post. "Nope," I said. "You heard Ma. Matt and Joey will send us what we need. It'll work out. I bet Joey and Matt will send enough for another duck." Philip's duckling had disappeared one night, eaten by a cat, no doubt.

"Pinky says the Czechs over in Ducktown buy feathers for pillow-making. Has to be duck feathers, not chicken," said Philip. "Every feather pillow in the whole world comes from ducks. And you can teach 'em to walk in a row, too," said Philip. His eyes were bright with excitement, and I noticed he'd gotten a few new freckles. "Pinky says they're smarter than chickens. If I sold some big bags of feathers, we could have sugar again," said Philip. He went off to feed the pigs while I closed up the henhouse for the night.

We watched as Mrs. Cimmermancek and Emmeline left the house. Ma waved and thanked them for dropping by. She waved until they were out of sight down the hill. Then she turned and called to us in Croatian.

"Slava! Filip! Come in now. Hurry!"

Philip brought the two empty slop buckets, one in each hand.

"Philip stinks, Ma!" I yelled. "Want me to make him wash up first?" Ma shook her head.

"Now. Come." She turned and went into the house.

Chapter Eleven

Good news," said Ma. We sat at the table with Ma and Mary. "Matt and Joey are fine. Matt sent us money—sixteen dollars. The work is good. Emmeline and her mother will travel . . . for the wedding," said Ma.

"They're not coming back here for Matt's wedding?" said Philip. His lip trembled a bit. Ma shook her head and blinked back the water in her eyes. "Everything is good news, but—" Ma hesitated. We waited to hear what she had to say. "Matt asks to keep it quiet for now."

"Are they eloping?" asked Philip.

"No, silly," said Mary. "There's a priest and a church. Everything is dandy."

If it was such good news, why did I feel frozen?

Why was Ma wiping her eyes? Why was Philip sniffing? Why was Mary so down in the mouth? Matt and Joey weren't coming back.

"Could I write a letter and send it to the lumber camp?" I asked.

"No," said Ma. She shook her head. "Not now."

"They . . . uh . . . move around, Cuss," said Mary. "Place to place."

I felt like someone had just dealt me a stiff uppercut. And the lumberjack story was starting to smell.

"Mama," said Mary, "I'm gonna quit work when I get married. What'll you do without my wages?"

"I can sell milk, butter," said Ma, "and, in the spring, three calves. I have ten dollars a year for my widow's pension. I'll save up and then I'll buy two more pigs. If the calves are heifers, I'll have three more cows."

"If Cuss went to work, you'd have enough for sure," said Mary.

"No," said Ma. "For now everything stays the same. I have decided." She stood up, went into the kitchen, and in no time we heard the rattle of pots and pans. I fetched my arithmetic book and spread out my homework on the table. I sent Philip outside to wash the slop buckets, and then I sat down to work on fractions.

I had to read the same problem half a dozen times before I was able to start. Ma washed dishes. Mary clicked her knitting needles. Soon enough I put aside all the thoughts and feelings that were plugging up my brain. Seven-fifths divided by thirteen-sixteenths times eighteen-nineteenths divided by two-thirds. I concentrated on the numbers and scratched with my pencil. The knitting needles stopped. Mary put a hand on my shoulder.

"You can't stay in school forever," she said. "That's the fact of the matter."

"I'm no miner," I said.

"Put a pickax in your hands and you will be," she said. "If Ma needs you to, you will, right?" Mary stood and messed up my hair with her hand. I blinked and blinked and stared at my homework. "Clement says a fellow gets used to working in the dark."

I sat as still as a statue, wishing my sister would go away so I could finish my work. Mary crossed the room and went into the kitchen. I squeezed my eyes shut and two big wet drops fell smack in the middle of my homework paper. I sopped them up with a corner of my sleeve and hoped they wouldn't show by the time I handed in my homework to Skunky.

It took a long time for me to fall asleep, and when I did, I dreamed I was trapped in a coal mine without any lamp. Everywhere I reached, I touched the rock. I hollered out for help, but it was just me in that black hole, alone and with nowhere to go.

I woke up to the clanging of the town hall bell. I sat straight up and my heart was going lickety-split. That bell only sounded for two reasons—a cave-in or explosion in one of the mines, or a fire somewhere in town. The sun hadn't come up yet, but I could tell by the sky that it was just beyond the hills. I listened and heard that it was the signal for fire—one ring and then a pause, then another ring. I got up and pulled on my overalls. Philip was awake by then, too.

"Fire bell," said Philip, sounding as relieved as I felt.

A cave-in was the nightmare of everyone who lived in Roslyn. And an explosion in the mine was even worse. A regular fire was bad, but not as bad as a mining accident.

"Probably one of the saloons," I said. The saloons caught fire regularly on account of all the cigar smoking that went on. Drunk fellows didn't always stub out their stogies before tossing them on the floor.

By the time we finished chores and breakfast, the commotion was over and it was time for school. I had almost forgotten my bad dream and everything that Mary had said the night before.

Chapter Twelve

Before taking the roll, Skunky rapped on her desk with a pencil to get our attention.

"Slava," she said, "please move forward in your row. Everyone else behind Slava, move up one desk also. I'm sorry to say that Percival won't be coming back to school."

Not coming back to school? I grabbed my things from under my desk and moved into Perks's seat. Skunky took roll and then started in on the lessons, but I might as well have been on the planet Mars. Where was Perks? It wasn't until lunch that I got my answer.

"His pa almost kicked the bucket this morning," said Skinny. "Didn't you hear?" I shook my head. "The whole town's talking about it. Didn't you hear the fire bell?" I nodded. "Old man Perkins was feeding the mules at the Number Five. One of them kicked the lamp out of his hand, and the glass broke and the kerosene caught the hay on fire. Perks's pop got it bad trying to save those mules. Burned his arms all the way to his chest.

"You know that new doctor?" asked Skinny. "Dr. Moody? Well, Mrs. Johnson told Ma that he was on the spot in less than five minutes, yelling at folks not to touch Mr. Perkins, and pretty much running the show. Mrs. Johnson said that if Perks's pop lives, he won't ever use his hands again."

I stared at Skinny. What would happen to my pal if his pa died?

"Tough luck, ain't it?" said Skinny. He scratched beneath the neck of his heavy wool sweater. It was still too warm for sweaters, but Skinny's ma always worried about pneumonia. "Genevieve Perkins told my sister, Helen, that their uncle Cedar came and took Perks to the Number Five today."

"What's he gonna do?" I asked, getting my voice box back into gear. "He's barely thirteen."

"Mules," said Skinny. "Like his pa. His pa got all the mules out, every one. Saved the company mules, but burned his arms to a crisp. Cuss, it makes me glad I'm gonna be a butcher."

"Yeah, lucky you," I said, but I was only listening with half an ear. Perks had sworn up and down that he'd never work for the mining company, but when a family needed money, what good was a dream? Now Perks would be tending mules, feeding and watering them and hitching them to coal cars. He'd be the first one to get to work and the last one to leave. He'd work in the dark all day.

A year back four mules and their skinner had been killed in a cave-in. It was dangerous, hard work and didn't pay as well as swinging a pickax. How could one boy do the job of a grown man?

I was in a dark mood when the principal rang the bell to end lunch. I didn't pay attention when Skunky announced that the new Latin teacher had arrived. I'd opened my English book and was reading the poem of the day for the second time when suddenly everyone stood up. I stood up, too, and when I looked I saw why. It was a priest.

"Class, please say good afternoon to Father François Duval."

The short, stocky priest bowed slightly. He took off his hat and cloak and hung them on a hook by the door. His black cassock was dirty around the bottom, and I could see that his boots were almost as old as mine. His black rosary beads hung from his belt.

He wore the same big Saint Benedict cross that our parish priest, Father Giroux, wore. That made him a Benedictine, probably from the Benedictine monastery and boarding school near the state capital, in Olympia.

Father Duval motioned for us to sit. Then he began to speak. "I am very happy to be here," he said. Like Father Giroux, he had a French accent. "I have been sent here to Roslyn to help Father Giroux, as he is not feeling well these days. I have just arrived today, on the train." I'd noticed how badly Father Giroux's hands shook during mass now, and how he often dozed during the Scripture readings. "In addition, I will come three times each week to teach you Latin." At this his dark brown eyes lit up and he shifted his weight to his toes, leaning toward us.

"Some say that Latin is a dead language," said Father Duval in a whisper. "How wrong they are! It is not dead. It is much alive. I will prove it to you. How many of you know some Latin already?"

All the Catholics raised their hands, which was about two-thirds of the class. Sure, we knew Latin. We could recite the Pater Noster or the Angelus or the Salve Regina backward and forward.

"Good," said Father Duval. "Very good." His hands were thick, and when he grinned, his large white teeth hung over his bottom lip in a comical smile. I'd say he was around thirty, but it was hard to tell with religious. "By high school you will all be reading Virgil and Augustine," said the priest. "Maybe sooner!" He leaned forward on his toes again and looked us over. "Why do we learn Latin?" he asked.

Clara Fontana raised her hand. "To pray?" she said.

"To pray if you are Roman Catholic," he said, "but that is not everyone, eh?"

Clara shook her head and blushed.

Father Duval leaned toward us. "Do any of you want to be a medical doctor?"

Freda Carlson raised her hand and everyone laughed. A girl doctor. What a joke.

"Very good," said Father Duval, ignoring our laughter. "Anyone who has a desire to study the natural sciences will need to know Latin. Everything is Latin!" He gestured broadly. "Botany, biology, medicine, nursing, pharmaceuticals, veterinary science—even the agriculturist has to know it! It is wonderful! Every plant, every animal, every muscle of the body—whether human or animal—has a Latin name. It is so useful! It is a universal scientific language. And it is also beautiful. The poetry, the great literature of the Roman Empire . . . almost as beautiful as French."

Father Duval was lovestruck with Latin. I'd only thought of Latin as something Catholic, like rosary beads.

"Do you remember I said Latin is not dead?" said Father Duval. "Oh, no, it lives on in its children. English is not a Latin language. It is Germanic, a cousin to German, yet sixty-five percent of English words have Latin roots, yes? So the English, they borrowed from Latin quite heavily. But you knew this already."

I didn't know it. I wondered if anybody else did.

"I feel a demonstration is in order," said the priest. *"Chiunque qui parla italiano?"* At first no one moved, but then Angela Andredtti's hand went up and others followed. Capelli, Valeri, Checci, Gargano; even Skinny put up his hand. More than half the wops admitted knowing Italian. Perella, Dulcina, and Constantini kept their hands down, but we all knew they spoke Italian by how well they swore. *"Meraviglioso! Sarete i miei allievi migliori,"* said Father Duval.

"What'd he say?" I whispered to Stinky Valeri, who sat to my right.

"Wops are smarter than bohunks," Stinky said.

I slugged him in the arm.

"Est-ce que quelqu'un parle français?" No hands. Father Duval's whole body slumped in disappointment and a couple of girls snickered. "Not one person speaks French? I may die of sorrow. *Español?*" No hands. *"Limba română?"* Three hands. *"Qualquer um fala aqui o português?"* No hands.

79

Father Duval looked us over. He hadn't stopped smiling. He dug in his cassock pocket and pulled out a pack of chewing gum.

"This chewing gum will go to the first brilliant student who can tell me the five beautiful modern languages that come to us directly from Latin."

I had never had a whole pack of chewing gum. My hand shot up. Skunky called my name.

"Slava Petrovich," she said. I swallowed. Three other hands went up. I had the first chance. Father Duval looked at me and nodded.

"Italian," I said. "And French." Father Duval grinned and rocked back and forth from heel to toe. Did the other kids realize he'd given the answers already? "And Spanish. Portuguese." I was positive about the last. I knew a few choice phrases in this one. "Romanian."

"Correct!" said Father Duval. "Think of Rome. And remember the five Romance languages."

He came down the row and handed me the chewing gum. I thanked him and put it away in my pocket. Everyone stared. I'd earned it fair and square and I felt as rich as Rockefeller.

"'Petrovich,' did she say?" asked Father Duval.

I nodded.

"*Laku noć,*" he said in Croatian, which got him a fair share of stifled giggles. "Did I say something wrong?" asked Father Duval with a half-grin. His eyes had a lively twinkle, like a kid who was up to no good.

"*Dobar dan,*" I said. "It's afternoon, so you say 'good afternoon.' *Laku noć* is 'good night.'" I felt my face turn red. Would I get in trouble for correcting a priest?

Father Duval nodded and repeated the greeting. "*Dobar dan.*" He said it to himself three times as he walked to the front of the classroom. "Thanks to Master Petrovich, my Croatian has improved." He turned around and folded his thick hands together across his wide chest. "You see, we all have much to learn, even the priest. I will correct your mistakes and you must correct mine, agreed? One must never cease from learning. We will learn together. *Multa sunt, quae mentem acuant,*" Father Duval said, then translated the Latin to English. "'Many things sharpen the wits.'" He motioned for us to repeat the phrase.

"*Multa sunt, quae mentem acuant,*" we said.

"What English word sounds like *multa*?" Skinny raised his hand.

"Joseph Giombetti," said Skunky with a nod in Skinny's direction. "Go ahead."

"Multiple," said Skinny. "And *molti* means 'many' in Italian."

"Brilliant!" cried Father Duval. "And what about the Latin word *mentem*?" There was a pause and then a hand.

"Mental?" said Clara Fontana.

"It is already happening!" said Father Duval, and he clapped his hands with glee. "Such sharp wits you have! You have discovered that *multa* is 'many things,' and *mentem* is 'mind,' or 'mentality,' or, as we say, 'wit,' and I didn't do a thing! You shall sharpen your wits even more with Latin. You will be fine Latin students. The finest. Until next time. *Au revoir!*"

Skunky thanked the new priest and handed him his cloak and hat. He waved at us just before he went out the door.

"Father Duval has brought Latin books, a gift to our school from Saint Martin's Academy."

She passed out the books and a couple of boys groaned out loud, but I wasn't one of them. I opened to the title page: *Bennet's Latin Series, First-Year Latin, Preparatory to Caesar.* I thumbed the pages and stopped at a drawing of a man's head. Underneath it said "Gaius Julius Caesar." I'd heard of Julius Caesar. I didn't know he knew Latin.

Chapter Thirteen

That night after chores I slipped away to see Perks. It had begun to rain and around seven the wind started up. Main Street was quieter than usual, probably because all the saloons had their doors shut against the storm.

When I got to the cafe, I went around to the back and knocked. The door opened and a dark brown eye with curly lashes peeked out at me.

"It's nothin' but Cuss," said Perks's little sister Molly Jeanette. She pulled the door open and let me in onto the back porch. "You smell like a wet dog," she said, holding up the kerosene lamp. "Don't drip all over."

I hung my coat and cap on a peg by the door. I knew where Perks was and headed for the small kitchen. I found him with his arms deep in hot water, washing a big soup pot.

"Hey, pal," he said. "Grab a dish rag."

"Nothin' doin'," I said and leaned against the sink. The one electric bulb in the kitchen didn't give off much light, but I could see Perks looked bushed. I reached into the water and splashed him. "We got a new Latin teacher," I said. "Father Duval. He's French."

"Yeah, well, I got me a bunch o' new teachers," he said. "There's Mudhole, Gimpy, Stubb, Whitey, Pisspot, an' Jake. They don't talk Latin, though, French neither. Just hee-haw."

"What's it like?" I asked.

Perks scrubbed the bottom of the pot. "Three bucks a day—that's what it's like. Eighteen bucks a week. And no more homework, Cuss. Now, that's sweet." He grinned and winked. Perks turned away and concentrated on the next pot. The smile slid right off his mug.

"How's he doing?"

"He'll live," said Perks. "Granny's been tending him. Doctor gave him morphine, so he don't feel much right now."

Perks put the clean pot on a table to dry, lugged the dishpan to the door, opened the door, and threw the dirty water outside. He brought the dishpan back inside, filled it halfway with water from the bucket on the floor, then took a big kettle off the woodstove and filled the dishpan all the way up with steaming water.

"See that stack of plates?" Perks nodded in the direction of another dishpan full of dirty dishes. "I got to wash all them and the cups, too, before the late-night customers show up, so I don't really have time to chew the fat."

"Hokey-dokey," I said. "I'll skedaddle. I wouldn't want to slow you down."

Perks seemed even scrawnier than usual. Maybe it was the long, dirty apron he had tied around his skinny middle. Maybe it was the slump of his bony shoulders. I dug in my pocket.

"Here," I said, holding up the pack of chewing gum.

"Where'd you get it?" asked Perks. "You swipe it from the company store?"

"Latin teacher gave it to me."

"Liar."

"Swear to God," I said. Perks wiped his hands on his apron. I handed him the gum.

"If they're handin' out treats at school now, guess I'm sorry for missin' it after all. I'll have to hide this from my sisters." Perks lifted his apron and stuffed the gum deep in his pocket.

"I'd better skedaddle," I said. "It's looking like a hurricane out there."

"Thanks for the gum," said Perks, and he held out his hand to shake. We shook and he smiled, but when he turned back to the dishpan, it was his eyes that were full of water.

"See you around," I said.

"Yeah, maybe I'll stop over to wrassle you."

"I'll paste you, Perks."

"Liar."

"Double liar," I said, and Perks smiled.

"Scram! Before I drown your ugly head in dishwater," he said.

"I'm leaving," I said, and I splashed him once more before heading toward the back porch and out the door.

The raindrops stung my cheeks. The wind blew right through my coat and wool trousers, and pretty soon the fronts of my legs were soaked. Perks wouldn't be by to wrassle, and we both knew it. Once a boy quit school and went to work in the mines, everything changed. Poor Perks. No mule skinner ever owned a Ford sedan.

Ma scolded me for being out in a rainstorm, but she ended her Croatian ranting with a hug and a kiss, a smack to the behind, and the last apple dumpling in the pantry. I stood by the stove while I ate, drying myself off, front and back, trying to shake the chill.

Fall was in full swing, and that meant getting ready for winter on top of schoolwork and all our regular chores. Ma paid three dollars for a ton of hay, which was delivered to our house on a Saturday afternoon. Uncle Tony came over with my cousins Bingo and Blacky to help me and Philip stack all the hay in the barn. If Matt and Joey had been around, we wouldn't have needed the extra help.

One week we picked apples so Ma could sell the good ones to neighbors. Four bushels earned her eight bucks. The next week it was carrots and beets and parsnips. Everything had to be picked, cleaned, sorted, and stored for the winter, and anything extra was sold.

After that Ma and Mary made sauerkraut. They shredded cabbage with the big kitchen knife, salting the layers and mashing them down into the kraut crocks. When our kraut crocks were full, Ma made kraut for the neighbors who didn't want to bother. That earned her a few bucks, too.

We got money from Matt and Joey three times. I don't know if it came by wire or in the mail. Ma never showed us an envelope; she just announced at supper that they had sent so many dollars. If there was a letter, she read it, but they always said the same thing. There was plenty of work, they were well, and they'd send money again when they could.

Wherever my brothers had gotten off to, it was a well-guarded secret, and no wonder. My brothers had run off from the Mob. Mum was the word, and no one was about to let anything slip to a kid like me, even if I knew I could keep my trap shut as well as anyone.

Every night Philip and I did our homework at the kitchen table. Sometimes it took me twice as long to finish because Phil needed so much help. Whenever I felt like telling the little squirt to pull his own weight, I remembered all the times Matt had helped me with my homework. I missed my brother. I wondered if he missed me.

Ma and Mary worked on wedding things in the evenings. Ma crocheted lace lickety-split, while Mary cut and sewed at the treadle Singer. No one talked about money, but there were signs that we'd begun to tighten our belts.

Three times Ma sent me and Philip out to the Number Seven slag pile to pick coal. It was one of the newer slag piles, and there was still a lot of coal mixed in with the rock, little pieces that the coal company didn't care about. We filled buckets and brought them home. It wasn't hard work but it was poor work. We'd always bought our coal by the ton.

We butchered a hog in late October, as soon as the temperature was down to stay. Ma woke us up long before daylight to do the job. Philip and I tied up the hog and led him out of the barnyard, where Ma, Mary, Uncle Tony, Uncle Andy, and Uncle Cyril were waiting. The pig's name was Hoofer, and I suspect he thought he was about to get fed. Instead, he got a smack between the eyes with a sledgehammer, and then Uncle Andy stuck him in the throat with Ma's long sticking knife.

Mary caught all the blood in a basin, while my uncles hoisted the carcass up off the ground with a rope and pulley hung from the limb of a big pine tree and got ready to scald the hog. By the time the sun was peeking over the hills, the hog was gutted and ready to scrape.

I'd played hooky in order to help Ma with the butchering, but so did lots of the kids when it was butchering weather. We all counted on Skunky overlooking the fact.

When I was little, Matt had taught me the names of all the guts of a hog, what they did, and what kind of meat Ma made out of them. Once when I was five, he paid me a penny to name all the parts. "What's that, Slava?" he'd say, and sure enough I knew. Liver, kidney, gallbladder. He'd bragged about me to our uncles and bet them a penny apiece that I could get all the names right. He won that bet, and gave me one of the pennies. Even looking at a pile of guts in the washtub made me miss my big brothers all over again.

Chapter Fourteen

Mary's wedding was on a Saturday, and all morning Ma was fit to be tied. "No snowballs and no fighting," she said. It had snowed the night before, and Philip and Pinky had already laid in a supply of snowballs out behind the barn. Ma was wearing her best black dress, the one with handmade lace that hung to the waist. "You get dirty, I kill you," she said in English. She put me in charge of keeping Philip clean, too, which I knew would be no cakewalk.

Hairy and some of his pals came by to get Matt and Joey's bed. Ma'd given it to Mary for a wedding present. I helped Hairy take the metal frame apart and carry the mattress and springs down from the attic, while Mary hid in the downstairs bedroom because it was bad luck for a groom to lay eyes on his bride before the wedding. I wondered what jokes Matt would have made on the wedding day of his only sister.

Ma wouldn't accept anything but a noon High Mass wedding, so by the final *Deo grátias,* I was on the verge of death from starvation. Fortunately, we ate for the rest of the day and well into the night. The Pinin' Miners played dance music. I thought of Matt and Joey missing all of this, but I didn't let it get me down for long.

All my cousins came to the wedding. We danced and chased each other and my necktie ended up in my pocket. Philip bumped Uncle Louis and got wine down the front of his shirt. By then Ma didn't care because even she'd had more than one glass of Uncle Tony's specialty. I ate until I had to let my belt out two notches. Emmeline said hello to me but I had a mouthful of raisins and could only blush and wave and wonder if Matt's wedding would be this much fun. I watched as she made her way toward a group of girls. No one knew she was going away to get married. How could she keep such a big secret?

All the men got drunk except for Uncle Andy, who was a teetotaler. Hairy got especially drunk, since it was his wedding. I hoped the shivaree would be a good one. Next to eating, the shivaree was the best part of any wedding.

Around midnight Mary and my new brother-in-law left to walk to their new house. Hairy'd built it himself. His brothers and relatives and bachelor friends walked along to keep them company. We boys followed at a distance. I counted sixteen cousins from our side of the family. The rest were related to Hairy.

We waited in the shadows, watching as Mr. Bovitz carried Mrs. Bovitz through the doorway. Hairy's friends said goodbye and wished the new couple luck. As soon as Hairy and Mary were locked inside, they joined the rest of us gathered around the house, as quiet as thieves. The Pinin' Miners had found their way to Hairy and Mary's house, too, with guitars and accordions and violins.

The moon was high, and the snow made it easy to see. Our feet and hands were numb, but we didn't care. Philip's teeth began to chatter until I elbowed him hard. My cousins and I jostled and shushed one another to keep quiet. It's a wonder Hairy didn't hear us sooner.

Finally the light went out. That was our signal. We started to scream like a bunch of banshees. Philip and I had sneaked two piss pots out of the house and stored them behind the church. Now we banged them together and hollered. My uncles and cousins were yelling and whistling. The Pinin' Miners played

"Ma! He's Making Eyes at Me," and then launched into "I'm Just Wild About Harry," singing in girls' voices and getting a great laugh. Our cousin Blacky banged on the side of the house with a log. Finally the light came on. Hairy came to the door.

"Get lost, you vermin!" he shouted. There was a wide smile pasted on his face.

Someone shouted "Shivaree!" and we all took up the chant. "Shivaree! Shivaree! Shivaree!"

"I said get lost!" yelled Hairy. "My baby doll's shivering in the bed." He winked and we all laughed. "Here," said Hairy, digging in his trousers pocket. "You kiddies go buy yourselves some candy."

I heard the rattle of coins. Hairy pulled out not pennies, the usual payment, but a fistful of nickels! He held them up for us to see.

"Back up!"

We all took a few steps backward and Hairy tossed the nickels into the air, scattering them on the hard-packed snow in front of his house. Then he threw a second fistful, then a third!

Philip and I dove and started grabbing for nickels. So did all the other boys. "There!" yelled Hairy. "I paid fair and square. Now, skedaddle!" He laughed, shut the door, and we all scrambled around looking for money.

Finally the band played "Ain't We Got Fun," and we left the newlyweds in peace. Hairy had paid well, better than anyone else before him. If he hadn't paid, he would have ended up running through the woods in his birthday suit, chased by the whole lot of us. Nickels was a fine way out.

My cousin Little Viktor got the most nickels— nine. I got thirty-five cents' worth, second place. Those nickels weighed down my trousers like lead fishing weights. Hairy was proving himself to be a dandy brother-in-law.

When I got home I lit a lantern, sat at the kitchen table, and wrote Matt a long letter all about Mary's wedding. I was feeling so fine that I wrote four pages on both sides. I told about the food and the wedding and how Ma had actually gotten tipsy. I told about the shivaree and the band and the thirty-five cents. When I ran out of wedding things to tell him, I told him about school, how we had a new Latin teacher, and how I was the best Latin student in class.

I didn't tell him Ma had sent us to pick coal. I didn't tell him how much I missed him. I stuck to good news and I thanked him for the money he'd sent. I wished he'd write back. I wished he'd tell me where he was. Matt knew I could keep a secret. No mobster would ever get the truth out of me.

I folded up the letter and put it in my coat pocket. Tomorrow at Sunday mass, I'd slip it to Emmeline with one of my nickels for postage. I'd tell her to keep the change. She'd send my letter to Matt. I felt sure she'd know how. I went to bed feeling like a king.

The next day I hurried to look for Emmeline at church, but she never showed up. At lunch Ma told me and Philip that Emmeline and her mother had left town on the morning train. She warned us not to spread it around, that if anyone asked we should say we'd heard they had gone to visit relatives in Spokane. Ma had fear all over her face, and for once I didn't feel so peeved that she hadn't let me in on the secret. She didn't want anything bad to happen to her boys. Neither did I.

I hoped Matt would have as good a shivaree as Hairy Bovitz had had. I hoped Emmeline had heard about the nickels and would tell Matt. Maybe Matt was so rich from cutting timber that he would throw dimes. Or maybe they didn't do shivarees wherever he was.

My favorite brother was getting married and we weren't going to be there to celebrate. After everyone went to bed that night, I put my letter in the cook-stove and watched it burn to ash.

Chapter Fifteen

I only saw Perks twice before Christmas, and both times he said he was glad he didn't have homework anymore. I knew it was just an act, but I went along with it. I told him his old desk was too small for me and that I'd found his initials carved under the lid.

"Yeah, and now I ain't around to get the strap for it, either," he joked. "Skunky can't touch me over at the Number Five."

I didn't tell him how much fun the Latin lessons were turning out to be or how Father Duval had told Skunky that he'd like to teach French to the eighth graders next year. I didn't tell him how I hoped and prayed that I'd be in school long enough to take French lessons.

Instead, we talked about which boys had quit

school, which mines were hiring, and who was leaving town to work in the shipyards or lumber camps. Perks bragged about earning a wage and said he was saving a dime a week toward a Ford sedan. I didn't say so, but even in hard times Ma'd always let Mary and the boys keep half their wages. Matt had saved up enough to get married. Joey probably had a stash himself. If Perks's ma was keeping all but a dime of Perks's wages, they were worse off than I'd figured.

At midnight mass on Christmas Eve, Bart Veranti and Skelty Sammich got in a fistfight just after the Credo. The fighting started out as a scuffle at the back of the church, and before long the ushers hauled them away and dumped them into the snow outside. Father Duval pretended not to notice and just kept right on saying mass.

I overheard someone whisper that the fight was on account of a card game, but right after mass Skinny said that Bart had gotten mixed up with a big Seattle bootlegging outfit. His pa had heard it from the barber that very morning. Skelty left town that night, took his wife and baby and skedaddled. Skelty was one of Matt's pals. I hoped he got far away.

On Christmas Day Mary and Hairy came for dinner. Hairy gave Ma a teacup that said "Nippon" on the bottom; to Philip and me, he gave one new dime and a peppermint stick each. Later Hairy whispered to me and Philip that there was a good chance we'd be uncles in August. Philip asked if we'd get cigars when we became uncles, and Hairy hauled off and tickled him until he yelled uncle.

On New Year's Day a bunch of our cousins came by to play in the snow. My cousin Rocky knocked out two of his front teeth sledding and got blood all over the snow in our yard. Philip said that later on Rocky got a beating for losing his teeth like that.

After New Year's Day came the Feast of the Kings—another trip to church. Now that I was learning Latin, I didn't mind it as much. I liked to listen and see what I understood without looking at the English in the missal.

Winter term started in January. I was halfway through seventh grade and no one had said another word about me quitting to go to work. I buckled down to my studies and told myself I was out of the woods, even though I only half believed it myself. So what if we were eating a lot of sauerkraut and potatoes? And coffee without sugar was fine with me.

By the first of February there had been three more fights in town. The new doctor was getting a reputation for sewing up knife wounds so well that they hardly made a scar. There were rumors aplenty.

One night a gang of bootleggers from Yakima

showed up two miles down the line in Cle Elum and thrashed half a dozen Roslyn boys who were doing business there. No one was killed, but two fellows got broken bones and the county hired a deputy sheriff.

Not long afterward Emmeline's mother came over and gave Ma a photograph of Matt and Emmeline in their wedding clothes. She also gave Ma fifteen dollars that had come with the photo. The photograph and the money weren't the big surprise. There was another photo. Joey had a sweetheart.

Ma passed the photo around at supper. Who'd have thought old Joey would find a gal? I was happy for him. Ma kept wiping the tears from her eyes with her dish towel, and I figured at first it was because she was happy. Philip filled me in at bedtime. Joey's sweetheart was a Spanish gal from Mexico, name of Veronica. Joey might as well have married a wop for all the upset it caused Ma. Poor Ma. She didn't understand how one of her boys could marry a girl who wasn't a Croat. In the Old Country it didn't happen that way.

Ma was weepy for a couple of days until Emmeline's mother told her that Veronica had two brothers who were priests. Next thing we knew, Ma was bragging to our aunts that we were going to have two priests in the family and that Veronica looked Italian, which wasn't so bad since the Holy Father was Italian, too.

No one had said a word about money, but it

wasn't far from my mind. If Joey took himself a wife, that would mean even less money for us.

When I got home from school the next afternoon, Philip met me at the door. I was so hungry I could have eaten a horse, but one sniff told me supper would be late. Nothing was cooking in the kitchen, and Ma was nowhere in sight.

"Where's Ma?" I asked Philip.

"In the barn," said Philip. His forehead was wrinkled with concern.

"What gives?"

"She said for you to get out there as soon as you came home."

When I got to the barn, I heard grunting and squealing, and I heard Ma's voice. "Hold still, you poor baby," she said in Croatian.

I pushed the door open and squinted, wishing my eyes would adjust faster to the darkness. Ma was in the pigpen.

"Thank God you're here, Slava," she said. "Come and help me."

Ma had tied two ropes around the sow's neck and had tied each end to opposite sides of the wall so the pig couldn't run away. The pig was sitting in the straw and Ma was trying to coax her to drink something from a bucket.

"The sow is sick," said Ma.

I could see and smell for myself before Ma said a word. The pig had the scours.

"She won't drink the medicine I made," said Ma. "And I even put in a cup of molasses. You hold her head up and I'll pour it into her mouth."

A full-grown sow is a big animal. If she'd been well, I wouldn't have been able to straddle her neck like I did. I could tell by the way her ears drooped that she wasn't up to fighting. I sat just behind the two ropes. Then I put my arms around her neck and pulled up. She didn't resist, but she did let out a squeal.

Ma wedged the lip of the bucket between the pig's teeth and started to pour. It looked like Ma's usual remedy for diarrhea, sweet water and ground river clay. As soon as the first gush of medicine hit the pig's mouth, she stood up and started to yank at the ropes. I sat on her even harder and Ma continued to pour. Finally the pig gave up the struggle and swallowed some of the medicine.

"There," said Ma. "Now you'll get better." She patted the pig's head and smiled, but I could tell by the look on Ma's face that she was fretful. A good brood sow produced a passel of piglets in a year. Ma depended on the pigs for meat and money both.

"I'll clean up," I said. The sow hadn't moved. I

untied first one rope and then the other. Ma watched for a minute and then she picked up the bucket.

"What will I do if I lose my pig?" asked Ma, but she wasn't talking to me. She turned and left the pigpen.

I shoveled the dirty straw into the barnyard and spread out new straw in the pig's stall. By the time I finished, it was dark outside, so I lit the kerosene lamp. I took care to throw the smoldering match into the snow outside.

The sick pig huddled in one corner of the pigpen, grunting and shaking with cold or fever; I couldn't tell which. I pumped a clean pail of water and brought it in, but the pig wasn't interested. I watched as her sides heaved up and down with each breath. Sometimes Ma's cures worked, sometimes not.

I whispered a prayer to Saint Francis. If anybody cared about a sick pig, it would be him. Then I squatted down beside the sow's head and scratched between her ears. Joey'd brought her home from the auction in Yakima. She'd given us one litter of twelve piglets and was tame as a dog. Now her head was hot and her snout was dry and she smelled like Ma's clay-water cure. Philip pounded on the barn door and yelled for me to come to supper. I blew out the lamp and hung it back on its nail.

I had a hard time studying that evening. I had a

big Latin exam the next day and I wanted to get a good mark, but I couldn't concentrate. Ma sat in her rocking chair and prayed on her rosary beads. The rocking and clicking of beads drove me batty. Philip did his homework without asking for help. He and I took turns checking on the sow throughout the evening. Once I got up in the middle of the night, but there was no change.

Early the next morning when I went out to milk, I found the sow dead. I ran in to tell Ma the bad news. She was stirring the polenta for our breakfast.

"God's will be done," she said. We hurried through the meal without talking. Afterward Ma sent Philip to get Uncle Andy and his three big boys. We tied ropes around the pig and dragged her out beyond the pasture, poured kerosene all over the carcass, and set it on fire. It would burn for days. We couldn't eat a pig that had died of a disease.

"At least she won't rot," said Philip. His breath was like fog in front of his face. "I hope the crows don't get to her." He sniffed and wiped away a tear. Losing a sow was a disaster, and even a little kid like Philip knew it.

I took the Latin test that day, but I knew I'd missed at least one question. It was hard not to think of the dead pig. Two days later Father Duval handed back our papers. I'd missed two. *Vrlo dobro* was written in Croatian at the top of the page: "very good." Getting two wrong didn't feel very good, but Father Duval's Croatian remark made me grin just the same.

Every time he taught our class, Father Duval asked me to teach him Croatian words and phrases. He asked Toivo Suivonen how to say things in Finnish. He checked his Italian with Skinny. We went along with it, even though most of us kids thought he knew enough languages as it was.

A few days later while I was at school, our other sow died of the scours, too. We'd always had pigs for as long as I could remember, just like we'd always had cows. Ma counted on selling pigs for cash every year. Now the pig side of the barn was empty. Ma was quiet and Philip wiped his nose on his sleeve more than once. Mary and Hairy came to visit, but it didn't cheer us one bit.

Hairy smoked and Mary and Ma drank coffee without talking. I worked on Latin adjectives. *Altus, fortis, felix, facilis, difficilis, similis: high, brave, fortunate, easy, difficult, alike.*

The next time we had to take a Latin test, I wouldn't miss a single word.

Chapter Sixteen

Just after Ash Wednesday we got a letter from Matt. Mary and Hairy were over for supper when Ma made the announcement.

Mary had just finished clearing the table when Ma said in English, "A surprise for everyone. A letter."

Ma handed Matt's letter to Mary, who read it out loud. The gist was that Emmeline was in a family way, and Matt wouldn't be able to send as much money as before. Matt said he was sorry and hoped Ma would understand. Then he made a joke about how he was certain Ma would find a way to scare twice as much milk from the cows and how her sows would probably have two dozen piglets apiece. Mary stared at the letter. Hairy rolled a cigarette. Ma sat down hard.

"Thanks be to the good God," she said in Croatian.

"I don't know why they couldn't have waited another year to get married," said Mary. "Golly, Ma, how'll you make ends meet?" Hairy put his hand on Mary's and shook his head very slightly. Mary clammed up.

"I told your brother when he left, to marry Emmeline, with my blessing, as soon as he was settled in the new job," said Ma. "It was time. He is a grown man. He deserves happiness. So does Yosip. I told them we would get by, and we will."

"Cuss, we'll be double uncles," said Philip.

Right then I didn't care about being a double uncle. I went over to the shelf and picked up my pencil and a paper I'd been working on. I sat back down at the table and stared at an essay I was writing on the Revolutionary War. Suddenly the letters blurred together.

The hens had quit laying because of the long nights. The cows were giving less milk because they weren't getting fresh grass. The food in our cellar was nearly half used up, and it would be months before we'd have anything from the garden again. The Northwest Improvement Company Store gave credit, but Ma was against it. She cooked less and we ate less and no one dared say a word. Ma had put on the ritz for Mary and Hairy, but still, it was only two potatoes each, pickled beets, a bit of bacon, and a whole lot of kraut.

"I could try to get a job for Cuss," said Hairy. "I could put in a good word with my boss."

"He's only twelve," said Philip. "He can't work."

"What do you know, Phil?" said Mary. "Cuss is big. He'd pass for fourteen."

"No," said Ma, and the talk stopped. Her eyes were filled with tears, but when she looked at me her face softened. She glanced down at my schoolwork and back at my face. "Not yet."

I felt a tug on my sleeve. "Time to close up the barn for the night," said Philip. He hopped down from his stool. "Come on."

"Philip, you do it tonight," said Ma. "One boy seven and a half years old can put three cows to bed." Philip looked at me, shrugged, and headed out to do the chores.

Mary stood up. "I'll do the dishes," she said.

"No, I'll wash up," said Ma.

Hairy stubbed out his cigarette on the bottom of his boot and dropped the butt into his empty coffee cup. "I imagine we ought to be getting home now, huh, Mary?"

Mary nodded and kissed Ma on the cheek. "See you around, Mama," she said. "Thanks for the swell supper. 'Bye, Cuss." She yanked my ear on the way by. Then she and Hairy let themselves out the front door.

Ma folded her arms and looked at me. "Your brothers, your sister, nobody likes school so much. But Slava? He likes." I nodded. "Is good," she said in her broken English. She smiled and switched to Croatian.

"It is good to love learning," said Ma, "and I am proud of you. Your father would be proud, too. He was a smart man. He taught me to read. Did you know that?"

"No," I said.

Ma stared beyond me like I wasn't there. "I was twelve when the marriage was arranged, thirteen when we married," said Ma. "My mother bought me a beautiful prayer book as a wedding gift, even though she couldn't afford it and she knew I couldn't read. She didn't want your father to think he'd gotten a girl from a cheap family, you see. Every week at mass I pretended to read the prayer book, but it didn't take long for your father to discover my secret. He laughed out loud and promised to teach me to read. That prayer book was my schoolbook." Ma smiled as she remembered. "I was a very good pupil," she said. "Very stubborn. None of my sisters could read, none of my friends either. It is the same prayer book I have today."

I knew the book well. It was small and thick with

a brown-velvet spine and two ivory angels on the front. It closed with a brass clasp. When I was a little squirt I'd begged to sit on Ma's lap and have her show it to me. It was one of her two treasures — that and a photograph of Ma and Pa on their wedding day. Ma's prayer book was the only book we owned.

I'd never heard the story of how Ma got the prayer book, and I'd never wondered how she learned to read or when. I didn't know Pa had taught her. I didn't remember much about Pa except that he was big and when he was drunk he laughed hard. I didn't remember that he'd known how to read.

I'd been reading since first grade. Ma hadn't learned until she was thirteen. No wonder she stumbled at times and asked what words meant when she read the Croatian newspaper.

"Ma, your prayer book has Latin in it," I said. "Latin on one side, Croatian on the other." Ma nodded. "I'm learning to read Latin. My marks are the highest in the class."

"Why read Latin? Do you want to be a priest, Slava?"asked Ma. Her face brightened up. "Praised be Jesus and Mary."

"I don't think so." The thought of being a priest had crossed my mind but never stuck. I didn't know what I wanted to be, except that I didn't want to be a coal miner.

"Every family should give a boy to the Church," said Ma. "I have four sons. One should wear the cassock. I hoped you would have a calling. You're my smart boy, and learning Latin, no less."

"Doctors have to know Latin, too, and scientists of all kinds. And knowing Latin helps if you want to learn other languages like French."

"I never needed any other language until I came to America," said Ma. "English is ugly and difficult, but you speak it perfectly! You are a good American, Slava. Americans need only English, unless they are priests — then they need Latin."

"I'm getting high marks in English, too, Ma," I said, steering the conversation away from the priest business. "And science. Even better than last year."

"I am so proud of you, Slava, but we are poor people." She shook her head. "For us, to read and write a little is all we need." I felt my heart slide down toward my half-empty stomach. "Do you want to be a priest, Slava?"

If Ma thought there was a Roman collar in my future, she'd do anything to keep me in school. I wished I could lie to her. She was watching me and waiting for my answer. Nothing would make her happier.

I shook my head.

"I'm pretty sure I don't have a calling, Ma," I said. Ma sighed and shrugged.

"Oh, well," she said. "A mother can hope, can't she?" I saw her bite her lower lip. She turned away and we sat there without saying a word for what seemed like a long time.

"There are lots of other reasons to go to school," I said, trying hard not to sound like I was begging.

"Don't listen to Mary," she said. "You can finish this school year, I promise. I never dreamed one of my children would be so well educated. Seven grades of school. No one in my family went to seven grades, not even my smart brother, Viktor. This year you can finish. Next year? I don't know, Slava. It depends. Perhaps when you are thirteen you would like to learn a trade? Maybe a mechanic for the railroad? But don't you worry. We'll find my smart boy a good job. And we will do what we have to do to get through this hard year. God will provide. Until June you stay in school. Then we'll see."

I looked at my hands and my pencil and my essay. Ma patted my hand. This was her gift to me, to be able to finish seventh grade, even though we were hard up for cash right now and the mines would hire me in a heartbeat.

I forced my face to smile.

"Thanks, Ma," I said. Ma's hand was rough and red and the skin on her knuckles was split open in several spots. I put my other hand on top of Ma's and squeezed. How could I tell her that seven years of school was not enough?

A couple of days later Ma did something that almost knocked me flat. She sent me down to the company store with a list. I ordered a hundred pounds of flour, a hundred pounds of potatoes, ten pounds of coffee, ten pounds of salt, twenty pounds of sugar, ten gallons of molasses, and two tons of coal. Ma'd told me to use store credit. We had never used credit before.

After the clerk took my order, he asked how we were going to pay.

"Store credit," I said.

"Name of the miner and which mine? Or is it railroad?" asked the clerk. He smiled and waited for my answer.

"No miner," I said. "We don't have any miners anymore, except my brother-in-law, Hairy Bovitz. My ma gets a widow's pension."

"No brothers?"

I shook my head. I felt my face turn red.

"Sorry," said the clerk. "Sorry, kid. You have to have a miner in the family to get store credit. It's the rules. Otherwise, there's no way for us to get our money."

I clenched my teeth. "We'd pay it back," I said.

"Can't help you, son," he said. "Ain't you got family that can help?"

I didn't answer him.

"The coal I can do. Wouldn't want you folks to freeze. Three dollars a ton. Think your ma can pay back six dollars, sonny?"

"Yes," I said. I signed my name without looking at the clerk. Then I grabbed Ma's list off the counter and left the company store without looking back.

When I got home I told Ma the whole story. She didn't say a word.

The coal was delivered the next day. The next time we got money from Matt and Joey, Ma sent me down to the store with six dollars. She didn't order anything else after that.

Chapter Seventeen

In March I turned thirteen. Philip pounced on me while we were still in bed and tried to give me thirteen swats on the behind, but I caught him and tickled him until he squealed. Ma made hotcakes and covered them in watered-down molasses. I gave her a hug afterward and told her I'd grown an inch right there and then on account of that fine breakfast. She smiled and swatted at me with a dish towel.

"Don't be late to school," she said.

That night Mary and Hairy dropped by. Mary handed me a package wrapped in brown paper and string. "Here's something for the schoolboy," she said. "A birthday present."

I untied the string and handed it to Ma to add to her ball of string. Then I unwrapped the package.

"A book?" said Philip. "What for?"

"For reading, you dope," said Mary. "Nice cover, huh, Cuss?"

"You bought me a book?" I asked. I'd never owned a book before.

"Yeah," said Mary. "It cost fifty cents, too. It was either that or a baseball. Clement noticed how much you read, so there it is."

"Hell's bells!" said Philip. "Four bits!"

"Clement got a raise," said Mary with pride in her voice. "He's a boss now, at the Number Five." Hairy grinned and nodded and Ma clapped her hands.

"Do you know a little colored mule skinner named Perks?" I asked.

Hairy scratched his bald head and thought. "Cedar's nephew?"

"That's right," I said. "If you get a raise, does that mean everyone else does, too?"

Hairy frowned. "I don't s'pose so," he said.

"When do mule skinners get raises?" I asked. Mary frowned at me. "Because my friend works real hard and he could use the money."

"I"ll ask about it," said Hairy, and I knew he'd keep his word.

"Finally, an important man in our family," said Ma in a jolly voice. Then she and Mary started talking at once in happy Croatian. Ma would likely scold me later for putting Hairy on the spot, but I didn't care. Pals stick up for each other.

I looked at my book: *The World's Greatest Poetry.* It was navy blue with the title stamped in gold on the spine. I opened it and saw what Mary had written in the upper right-hand corner:

To Cuss, the only boy in this family with brains, on the occasion of your thirteenth birthday. Good thing you're smart enough to understand these poems, because they're gobbledygook to me! Ha-ha!
Love,
Mary and Clement, 1926

Philip leaned against me and whispered, "You can rip out the pages when the Sears Roebuck catalog runs out. I won't tell Mary."

"If you touch this book I'll brain you," I said.

"A baseball would have been better," said Philip. I yanked his ear hard enough to make him howl.

My own book. I didn't care what it was about. I leafed my way through it and looked at the crisp white pages and the dark print. The smell of the ink made my nose twitch. Matt would have said it was a dandy.

I wondered if he remembered it was my birthday.

That night after everyone was in bed, I went back

downstairs and found Ma, sitting by the stove. She was crocheting. When I got close I saw she was making a lace christening gown. She laid the work in her lap and reached for my hand. "Do you like the book?" she asked. "Mary told me she was going to buy you one."

"It's grand," I said, squatting beside her chair so my face was level with hers. I swallowed and opened my mouth. "Ma, if I gave you the three pennies for a stamp, would you send a letter to Matt for me?"

Ma looked away. "I don't send letters," she said. "It is too—"

"Dangerous?" I finished her sentence. Ma nodded. "Ma, where are they?" I waited for her to answer me, at least with a nod, or the shake of her head, but she didn't move and she didn't speak for a good minute.

"Go to bed, Slava," she whispered. "And don't forget your prayers."

I went to bed but I didn't feel much like praying. Instead, I lit the kerosene lamp and opened up my poetry book and began to read a poem by a fellow named Thomas Moore:

Oft in the stilly night
Ere slumber's chain has bound me,
Fond Memory brings the light

118

Of other days around me:
The smiles, the tears
Of boyhood's years,
The words of love then spoken;
The eyes that shone,
Now dimm'd and gone,
The cheerful hearts now broken!
Thus in the stilly night
Ere slumber's chain has bound me,
Sad Memory brings the light
Of other days around me.

It was only the first verse. It had a good sound to it. I read it again. Even though some of the words were dopey and old-fashioned, it made sense just the same. I read it over until I could recite it with my eyes shut. Then I closed my poetry book and blew out the lamp.

I pulled the covers up to my chin and thought about how much had changed since Matt and Joey had gone away, how nothing would ever be the same. That was what that poem was about, wasn't it? I stared across the room to where Joey and Matt's bed used to be until my eyes got heavy and my thoughts about my brothers turned into dreams.

Chapter Eighteen

Palm Sunday marked the beginning of Holy Week, which meant lots of church and a few days of vacation. The snow was all but melted and I was in a jolly mood as I did my evening chores. I had my poetry book with me, thinking I could take in a line or two as I milked. The days were longer now and we could milk at night without a lamp.

I'd found Philip a stray kitten. He'd named it Lucky despite the fact that it was black and gave Ma the willies. Lucky liked to hang around the barn. I was just about to aim a stream of milk at its mouth when I looked over and saw Philip leaning against Geraldine's swollen side. All three of the cows were due to freshen in late May and they weren't giving much milk. We'd milk them for another week and then let them dry up until their calves were born.

Philip's face was pale. He'd stopped milking but hadn't moved from his stool.

"What's wrong with you, Phil?" I said.

"My head hurts," he said.

"You trying to get out of work, squirt?"

"No," said Philip.

"Go on into the house," I said. Philip's eyes looked like burned holes in a gunnysack. "I'll milk all of the cows."

"You sure, Cuss?" he asked. Even his voice seemed pale.

"Yeah, I'm sure," I said. Philip stood up and wiped a hand across his face. "Go on, skedaddle." I closed my book, stuck it into my back pocket, and finished my own milking, then did Philip's.

When I got into the house, Ma was wrapping a wool sock around Philip's neck. Ma's cure for sore throat was a hot, wet wool sock covered by a dry wool sock, held together with a safety pin. It was itchy and soggy and hot, but sometimes it worked. Philip sat quietly on the stool and didn't resist. Usually he fought the wool-sock treatment and let everyone know what he thought about it, but this time he didn't make a peep. His face was as white as a piece of paper, and there were tiny beads of sweat on his upper lip.

"Up to your bed," said Ma in a cheerful voice, but I could tell by the look on her face that she was anything but. She helped Philip down from the stool and led him upstairs.

Every year some kid in town died from a disease that started with a sore throat. Two of our cousins and my brother Marko had died from scarlet fever, but they were babies and it had happened before I was born. Ma never talked about Marko. It was Matt who'd told me about him.

When I was in first grade, there was a diphtheria epidemic, and some of the houses over in Ducktown were quarantined. The doctor came into our classroom wearing a cloth face mask and looked down every kid's throat. No one in our class got sent home, but it turned out that three kids in the second-grade class had it, and one of them died.

A sore throat by itself wasn't anything. We all got those from time to time. It was the sore throat and high fever that made all good Catholic mothers get out the wool socks and warm up the rosary beads.

Ma came down the stairs. Now her face looked pale, too. "It's cold upstairs," she said. "And Philip is too sick to walk anymore. Slava, bring him down to my room." Ma bit her lower lip and then I heard her whisper, *"Neka nas Bog pomogne." God help us.* Her prayer sent a shiver up my backbone.

I took the stairs three at a time. I squatted beside our bed and patted Philip's shoulder. "Hey, squirt," I said, "Ma wants you downstairs again."

Philip opened his eyes, and then closed them. "My head," he whispered. "If I move it hurts too much." Tears squeezed out from the corners of his eyes. I'd seen my brother lose a toenail, cut his finger to the bone with a jackknife, and knock himself out against a tree playing ball, but until that night I'd never seen him cry tears of pain. I pulled back the covers and scooped him up. He put his hot arms around my neck. He shivered even though he was burning with fever. I carried him down the stairs and laid him on the bed.

Ma leaned over and felt Philip's cheek with the back of her hand. Then she looked at me and said, "Stay out so you don't get sick, too." Ma sat beside Philip and began to wipe his head with a damp cloth. "And say a prayer," she whispered.

I tried to study but it was impossible to think. Now and again Philip would whimper and I'd hear Ma talk to him and then he'd settle down. Every time it happened, it got my heart going full speed ahead. Finally I gave up on my schoolwork, went upstairs, stripped, and got into bed. I fished around under the blanket on Philip's side until I found what I was look-ing for. Ma's rosary beads, the ones she'd gotten for First Communion back in the Old Country, were under Philip's pillow.

At the first sign of sickness, Ma always put her special rosary under our pillow. The beads were clear glass, cut to look like diamonds. She said that if we were too sick to pray, the angels would pray for us. I fingered the old silver crucifix.

Skinny always had his rosary on him. His mother didn't let him leave the house without it. Mine was hanging on a nail in the closet. When I was little, angels, devils, saints, Jesus, Mary and Joseph—they were all as real as the aunts and uncles and cousins I could touch. Now I was thirteen and questions had begun to crowd my head.

Ma prayed all the time, but what good did it do? I'd prayed that the pigs wouldn't die, but they did. Maybe the problem was me. Maybe I didn't pray enough. If I prayed more, maybe my prayers would get all the way to heaven and bad things would stop happening to us.

The floorboards were hard and cold. I shivered and felt a wave of guilt. Was God trying to tell me something? Maybe this was my punishment for not praying enough. If I had more faith, I would pray like Ma said, and maybe Philip would get well. If I had more faith, maybe I'd want to be a priest, and then I could finish school for sure. But if this was a punishment, why was it Philip, not me, who was sick?

I let Ma's rosary slip through my fingers and drop onto the bed. I didn't want to be a priest. If I said I did, it would be a lie, and then I'd break the Eighth Commandment. I lay back and stared at the ceiling.

Primus, citimus, ultimus, proximus.

First, nearest, farthest, nearest.

Posterior, exterior, inferior, superior.

Later, outer, lower, higher.

There was a big Latin test scheduled for the Tuesday after Easter. If I couldn't pray, at least I could study.

Spero, dubito, erro.

I hope. I doubt. I am mistaken.

I slept hard that night and dreamed of Latin. Then I heard Ma's voice and I jumped.

"Slava?" she called. I jerked on my overalls and ran downstairs. I heard the town clock chime five o'clock.

"I'm up, Ma," I said. I got halfway across the sitting room and stopped. The light was on in her room and I could see Philip lying across the bed. Ma was hunched over him, holding him in her arms, or was she holding him down? I could hear him choking.

"What's wrong?" I asked.

"Get the doctor," said Ma without turning around. "The new doctor. Philip is having fits." I was out the door and running down the road before you could say "Yankee Doodle."

I'd been wearing boots all winter and my bare feet weren't hardened yet. I winced every time I hit a stone, but I didn't slow down. The only thing that ran through my head was *Help us, Holy Jesus.*

Chapter Nineteen

Dr. Moody, the new company doctor, came with me right away, black bag in hand. The talk about Dr. Moody was all good, but Ma wasn't keen on doctors, not even one who'd been to a fancy medical school out east. Ma and the other Old Country women had their own cures for nearly everything. I'd never been to the doctor in my life. I couldn't remember a doctor ever coming to our house. Any time someone died at the Cle Elum hospital, Ma blamed the doctors.

Ma wouldn't call for the doctor unless she was scared to death.

"How old is your brother?" asked the doctor. He was a young man, probably not yet thirty. I wanted to run, but could he keep up? Maybe it wasn't proper for doctors to run.

"Seven," I said, stepping up my pace. "Almost eight."

"And how long has he been sick?"

"Just today, I think," I said, but I wasn't sure. Had Philip looked pale earlier? Had he complained? Why hadn't I paid more attention to the squirt?

"What has your mother tried so far?"

"She puts a wool sock around our necks for sore throat," I said. "We're almost to my house." I hurried ahead, not wanting to explain Ma's cures.

When we got to the house, the lights were on. I could hear Philip crying. Dr. Moody crossed the sitting room and went into Ma's bedroom. Philip was lying in bed, wrapped in a soaking-wet bedsheet, Ma's cure for high fever.

"I wrap him," said Ma in English. Philip shivered and wept. Ma stroked his forehead. Her face was grimmer than I'd ever seen it.

Dr. Moody asked her questions while he got out a thermometer and shook it hard. I strained to hear, in case Ma needed a translation, but she understood his questions and answered him quietly.

"Hey, little fellow," said the doctor to Philip. "Can you open your mouth and let me take your temperature?" Philip opened his red, watery eyes and nodded.

"Under the tongue and keep it there. Hokey-dokey?" Philip nodded again and opened his mouth. The doctor took out his pocket watch. After what seemed like an hour, he took the thermometer from Philip and held it up to the light.

"One hundred and three," he said. "Still high, but not dangerous right now. Let's get him out of that sheet and into some dry clothes, all right, Mother?"

Ma nodded and the doctor left the bedroom.

"What's your name?" the doctor asked me. His eyes were bright blue, like the top of the sky on an August afternoon, and his teeth were too big for his mouth, but his smile was kind.

"Slava," I said. "But everyone calls me Cuss."

"On account of your being a mean cuss?" asked the doctor. His eyes twinkled.

"No, on account of . . ." I hesitated and felt my face turn red. "I'm good at swearing. In different languages."

"How many different languages?" asked the doctor.

I looked up and now he was grinning hard. "Fourteen," I said, "so far."

"Impressive," said the doctor, and then he winked.

"Should I do something?" I asked. Dr. Moody glanced down at my feet and frowned.

"You can let me look at that," he said. I looked down and saw a smudge of blood on the floor where I'd been standing. One of my feet was cut and bleeding. I must have stepped on something sharp when I was running to get the doctor. Why hadn't I noticed before?

When Ma came out of the bedroom, Dr. Moody was picking bits of gravel and dirt out of the cut. I wanted to holler but I kept my mouth shut. I gritted my teeth.

Ma pulled up a chair beside the doctor. "I do that now," she said, taking a bottle of iodine and some cotton from the doctor. "You see Philip, please."

Dr. Moody poured clean water over his hands into a basin, scrubbed with soap, and dried his hands on a towel. Then he left us and went to check on Philip.

Ma swabbed my foot in silence. "I can do it, Ma," I said. She shook her head.

"My boys," she said in English. "My boys." It was all I could do not to squirm away like a garter snake on a stick. She grabbed my big toe and wiggled it playfully. "Hold still," she said with mock sternness. "Almost finish." She swabbed an especially tender place.

"Yowch!" I said.

Ma's eyes filled with tears. "There is much sorrow with love, Slava. Much sacrifice."

I swallowed hard and wished she would finish up. I didn't want to hear about sorrow and sacrifice. Ma wrapped the bandage around my foot and tied it on top.

The rooster crowed and I looked out the window to see the first rays of sunlight creeping over the hills. The doctor came out of Ma's bedroom.

"I'm not sure what is troubling little Philip," said the doctor. "The fever can come from any number of illnesses."

"Diphtheria?" asked Ma. Her eyes were huge.

"Possibly," said the doctor. "But we haven't had any of that this year, thank God, so I'm doubtful."

Ma let out a sigh and crossed herself.

"The wet sheet brought the fever right down, but now I'm going to leave you some aspirin for Philip. One tablet every four hours. That should keep him from convulsing again. You mustn't give him more than one at a time, and not closer together than every four hours. Is that clear? It's very important." Dr. Moody glanced at me and I nodded to make sure he knew I would explain to Ma in Croatian if she didn't get it all. "Let's cross our fingers and hope that Philip will be able to fight the infection, whatever it is. We will have to wait and see. I don't have any way to tell what the germ is at this point," said the doctor. "I can only judge by the symptoms as they appear."

"Not diphtheria?" said Ma.

"I don't think so," he said, "but I could be wrong. Your little boy isn't out of the woods. Let him rest, give him sugar water and broth. Send for me if he worsens."

Ma thanked Dr. Moody and pulled a fifty-cent piece out of her pocket.

"Here," she said, holding it out to the doctor. "I pay." Dr. Moody shook his head.

"The mining company pays me," he said.

"I got no miners," said Ma. "Not until Slava works. I don't need no charity. Take the pay."

"Are you a miner's widow?" asked Dr. Moody, looking at me.

"Yes," said Ma. "Almost eight years a widow." The doctor turned to Ma and smiled.

"Then you and the children are covered," he said. "And that's that."

"Hvala," whispered Ma. *Thank you.*

Ma and I saw Dr. Moody to the door. I limped along on my bandaged foot, which was really smarting by this time. Just then Philip called out and Ma excused herself, hurrying to the bedroom. She had the glass bottle of aspirin pills in her hand.

Out on the front porch Dr. Moody put his hand on my shoulder. "What grade are you in, Cuss?" he asked.

"Seventh," I said.

"I hope you will take this in the spirit it is meant," said the doctor. "Do you know what I mean when I say that sometimes the immigrant folks are reluctant to ask for the doctor?"

"They have their own cures," I said, hoping Ma didn't overhear.

"Precisely," said the doctor. "And they also wisely know that there are those who call themselves doctors but are in fact quacks who sell useless and even harmful cures to poor people." I nodded. The newspaper was full of ads for elixirs of this or that, guaranteed to cure everything from baldness to nerves. "I'm not that kind of doctor," said Dr. Moody. "And I understand how desperate your mother felt to send for me. My grandparents came from Ireland. They still have a hard time trusting a doctor, even their own grandson."

"Ma says they didn't need doctors in the Old Country," I said.

"But this is America, and you're a smart boy, and I am going to count on you to help your brother, just as you did a few hours ago." Dr. Moody's grip on my shoulder tightened. He looked me in the eye. "Any one of four things should send you running to fetch me again, day or night," he said, "this time with something on your feet." I felt my face turn red and

133

nodded. "If he convulses again, if he has any stiffness or pain in his neck, if the light hurts his eyes, or if he can't keep water or food down for more than six hours, come get me straightaway. Can you remember those four warning signs?"

"Yes," I said. "I'm good at memorizing."

"Ah, yes," he said, smiling at me with his mouth crammed full of teeth. "You can cuss in fourteen languages." His bright blue eyes were tired and he needed a shave. The stubble on his chin was reddish blond.

"I'll keep an eye on Phil," I said. "It's Holy Week, no school."

"I'm counting on you," said the doctor, "but don't spend too much time in your brother's room. The sickness may be contagious." He gave my shoulder one last squeeze, then turned to walk down the steps. I spoke when he got to the bottom one.

"Dr. Moody," I said.

He turned around, his bushy eyebrows raised in question.

"Do you know Latin?" I asked.

"Why, yes," said the doctor. "Yes, I do. It was one of my favorite subjects."

"Mine, too," I said. "Thanks for coming."

"You're very welcome," he replied. "It's been my pleasure. You see, I feel that medicine is my calling. Sort of like being a priest."

"Vocamur," I said. "It's on the next Latin test."

Dr. Moody grinned and bowed at me. "We are called," he translated. "Very good. Yes, we are all called to something, aren't we? Keep that cut clean until it heals."

I told him I would, then I watched him walk away from the house and down the hill toward town.

Ma gave Philip the aspirins just like Dr. Moody had said, but she altered his prescription of broth and sugar water. At our house, sick kids got sauerkraut juice and hot, black coffee, and there were some things Ma wasn't about to change.

Philip didn't perk up, and the fever never left him. On Tuesday he complained that his neck hurt. When Ma opened the shade to let the light in so she could take a good look down his throat, he cried out in pain at the brightness. In two shakes I was running down the hill to bring Dr. Moody back to our house.

Chapter Twenty

Dr. Moody examined Philip again. When he came out of the bedroom, I could see Ma sitting beside Philip with her face buried in her hands. Mary had just stopped by. She stood near me as we waited to hear. I swallowed hard. "What is it?" I asked, and my voice squeaked a little.

"Meningitis," said the doctor, "an infection of the fluid that surrounds the brain and spinal cord." His shoulders were slumped and his bright blue eyes had lost their twinkle. "I'm sorry. I can't do anything more."

"Is he going to die?" whispered Mary, her lower lip trembling. I tried to swallow, but my throat was too dry.

"Children are surprisingly resilient," said Dr. Moody. His words said one thing, but the sound of his voice said another. "It would be best if you and Cuss stayed out of the room."

Mary's face screwed up and tears poured from her eyes in two streams that dripped off her chin. For the first time I noticed the bulge that would be my nephew or niece, and I remembered how tickled Phil had been about becoming a double uncle. My ears rang and my head felt thick.

"Should I do something?" I asked. My voice cracked. I cleared my throat. Dr. Moody put his hand on my shoulder and squeezed.

"You should fetch Father Duval," he said. "Don't wait."

Mary sobbed out loud. All I could do was nod, dash out the door, and run full speed to the church.

Father Duval was eating his lunch in the rectory, but when I told him we had an emergency, he came without a word, grabbing his purple stole and flinging it around his neck as he rushed out. Even though his legs were short, I had to break into a trot to keep up with him. Some of the neighbors saw us and followed along behind. A priest in a hurry could only mean one thing. Father Duval went into our house without knocking. I followed close on his heels.

Ma had lit candles and taken her big Old Country crucifix off the wall. It was propped up at the head of the bed where Philip lay small and pale, sweating and whimpering in his misery. Mary and I watched from the bedroom doorway as Father Duval put his hand on Philip's head, and Philip opened his eyes. They were watery and red, and even the dim light of the dark bedroom seemed to hurt them. When he saw who it was leaning over him, Philip made a tiny cry of surprise.

"Hello, my dear Philip," said Father Duval in a gentle voice.

"Am I gonna die?" whispered Philip. His voice was as weak as a sick kitten's meow.

Mary stifled a sob. I held my breath.

"Perhaps," said Father Duval. He picked up one of Philip's hands and patted it. "If you do, you will be ready to meet Saint Peter at the gate." Father Duval smiled. "And if not?" The priest shrugged. "Then you will not have to dress up in a suit and tie on First Communion Sunday next month like all of your poor classmates, for I am going to give First Holy Communion today, and Confirmation as well. Would you like that?"

Philip closed his eyes and nodded.

Father asked to be alone with Philip for a minute, but I doubted the little squirt would be making much

138

of a confession in his present condition. He hadn't lived long enough to do much more than cuss or swipe food from the pantry.

Soon Father Duval called Ma back in and she knelt beside the bed. Ma cried quietly, her hands clasped around her rosary beads. Mary and I knelt just outside the door. Father Duval started with the Pater Noster. I said it along with the rest, but I didn't listen to a word of it. I smelled the burning candles and felt the hard floor against my knees. I squeezed my eyes shut but not because I was praying. I squeezed them hard and opened them again, half hoping it was all a wretched nightmare.

After some more Latin words, Father Duval drew a golden pyx from his cassock pocket and took out a consecrated host. *"Corpus Christi,"* he said.

Then I heard Philip whisper, "Amen."

Father Duval broke off a crumb and placed it on Philip's tongue.

Viaticum was the Latin word for Holy Communion when a person was dying. We'd learned it in catechism class. It meant "food for the journey."

Philip's First Communion might be his last.

Now Father Duval placed his hand on Philip's forehead and prayed. I could see his lips moving, but I didn't hear what he was saying. He then took some holy oil and used it to trace the sign of the cross on Philip's head. "Philip, *signo te signo crucis et con-firmo . . .*" Father Duval said the words in Latin, but I understood them as if they were plain English. *With the sign of the cross I confirm you.* There was more Latin, more anointing with oil, and Philip had received last rites. Now all that was left was to pray.

"*In nómine Patris, et Fílii, et Spíritus Sancti,*" said Father Duval.

In the name of the Father, and of the Son, and of the Holy Ghost.

Ma wailed.

"*Miserére mei, Dómine, quia infírmus sum,*" said Father Duval.

Have mercy on me, Lord, for I am sick.

"*Sana me, Dómine, quóniam conturbáta sunt ossa mea.*"

Heal me, Lord, my bones are racked with pain.

Mary sniffled beside me. Ma was bent over double with grief. I felt the pain of kneeling on the hard floor as I did battle with the tears that wanted to spill out of my eyes. I wished Matt were there.

Aunt Katja slipped into the sitting room along with our spoiled-rotten twin cousins, Mildred and Margaret. They all knelt and joined in the prayers. Father Duval's voice droned on in the litany of the saints. I choked when I tried to say the responses. I looked at my little brother. He was such a squirt. Where was his guardian angel now? What good were all of Ma's prayers if this was how it was going to end? I wiped my nose on my sleeve.

Uncle Tony let himself in the front door and knelt, too, along with Putzy, who was sporting a bright purple shiner under his left eye. I glanced around the sitting room and was surprised to see other neighbors and relatives, sitting, waiting for my brother to die.

Father Duval finished and we all said, *"Deo grátas."* *Thanks be to God.* I crossed myself and got up, making my way through the crowd. Thanks be to God for what?

I heard Skinny's voice. "Hey, Cuss," he said, but I ignored him and kept going until I was out the back door, down the steps, and heading straight for the barn.

The cows were penned because they were close to freshening, and Ma didn't want them dropping their calves in the pasture. Geraldine was munching hay in her stanchion. I got out the milking stool and set it on the ground beside her. I didn't have a bucket, and she gave me a look, but then went back to chewing and ignored me.

I pressed my face against Geraldine's swollen belly and thought how good she smelled, not like the candle wax and sick smell of the bedroom I'd just left.

I heard the gurgle of Geraldine's gut and felt her calf moving inside. Geraldine had always been Philip's favorite cow.

I put my face in my hands and cried until my eyeballs ached.

Chapter Twenty-One

Ma stayed by Philip's bedside for two days and nights. She wouldn't let me or Mary come anywhere near Philip. Our aunts and the neighbor ladies took turns watching, worrying, and crying with Ma. They brought food and tried to get Ma to eat, but she refused anything but water or coffee. Dr. Moody visited every day, but there was nothing for him to do but wait with the rest of us.

I was a complete good-for-nothing. I couldn't eat, couldn't sleep, couldn't give my lessons a thought. Day and night felt the same. It was springtime and the sun was beginning to warm things up, but our house was cold and dark, and when we spoke we whispered.

On the third day after he had received last rites, Philip asked for something to eat, and quick as a wink it felt like Christmas Day around our house, even though it was Good Friday and we were supposed to be solemn. Seems the squirt had pulled a fast one on the Grim Reaper. Ma was all smiles despite her tiredness. Every other sentence that came out of her mouth was "Thanks be to God." Dr. Moody grinned so hard when he examined Philip that I thought his face must hurt.

On Easter Sunday I felt so happy that it seemed maybe I had some faith after all. We had Philip back. That was what mattered most.

Philip didn't get out of bed for a full two weeks, and when he did, he was as weak and pale as a baby. I got up extra early each morning and did his chores as well as my own. Now that his fever was gone, Mary came by every evening to sit with Philip while Ma and I planted the garden.

Matt and Joey sent money. It was less than usual, but all Ma said was "Thanks be to God." The power company shut off our electricity, but it didn't matter much. We only had the two lightbulbs—one in the kitchen and one over the dining-room table—and kerosene was cheap.

One night Geraldine had her calf. The whole thing went without a hitch. It was a bull calf. I told Ma. I knew it wasn't what she wanted to hear. Ma wanted heifers so she could raise them to be milk cows.

"I'll sell it for veal," she said.

Daisy and Bernice had their calves while I was at school the next day. One was a bull calf. The other was a heifer.

"Better than nothing," said Ma, but I could tell how disappointed she was.

By the end of April Philip was up and around, but the sickness had taken its toll. His face was thin and white and he got tired just walking to the outhouse and back. I didn't care a whit that he wasn't pulling his weight around the house. I figured when he was up and at 'em again he'd make up for it, but for the time being all I wanted to do was coddle him. It was my way of thanking him for not kicking the bucket.

Even though Philip was on the mend, Dr. Moody still stopped by almost every day. One afternoon he called me aside as he was leaving the house.

"I have something you might enjoy, Slava," he said. He handed me a thick black book. "I know you're a Latin scholar."

I opened the book to the title page and read: *Gray's Anatomy.* I thumbed through and saw dozens of drawings of the human body. There were veins and muscles and skeletons and organs. I'd seen plenty of butchered animals, but never the innards of a human.

"Each part of the body has a Latin name," said the doctor. "And they're very sensible and easy to remember if you like this sort of thing. For instance . . ." He took the book and flipped through it to a certain page. Then he handed it back to me. "See this picture? This is the underside of the human skull." He pointed with his finger. "Do you see what the name of the hole at the bottom of the skull is called?"

"*Foramen magnum.*" I thought for a second and then translated the words. "'Great hole'?"

"Exactly," said the doctor with a chuckle. "Isn't that delightful? It sounds so lofty, but all it means is 'big hole.'" I nodded as I read the other labels.

"Mandible is the jaw bone?"

"Yes, that's right."

I stared at the drawings. "It's swell," I said.

"I thought you'd like it," said the doctor. "So I'll let you borrow the book until I need it back. It'll help you with your Latin, I'm positive."

"I'll take good care of it," I said. "Thanks, Dr. Moody."

He headed down the hill whistling a little tune. I carried that book into the house and put it with my poetry book next to my side of the bed. That night I started at page one and began to read. Before I knew it, Ma called up to me to blow out the lamp and go to sleep. For a long time I lay in the darkness and thought about that book. When I finally fell asleep, I dreamed of tibias, ulnas, and latissimi dorsi.

A couple of nights later I was hoeing the garden when I noticed Philip sitting on the porch with his hands over his ears and a look of pain on his face.

"Phil!" I hollered. He didn't look up. I waved. "Hey, squirt!"

He kept his hands over his ears and shook his head. I dropped my hoe and ran over to him, calling out for Ma to come quick.

Philip rocked himself back and forth. His eyes were closed tight. I touched his shoulder. "What's wrong, pal?"

"My ears," he said. "They're ringing something awful." I let out a sigh of relief. At least it wasn't the headache.

"Maybe Gina Pallagrutti's telling one of her girl-friends that she's sweet on you," I said. I shoved him playfully in the shoulder, but he didn't respond.

"It's so loud I can hardly hear you."

By that time Ma was on the porch beside us.

"You head hurt?" she asked Philip.

"No," he said. "It's my ears."

"He says they're ringing," I said to Ma.

She frowned. "But no hurt?" she asked Philip, who seemed not to hear her. Ma looked at me with worry and a question in her eyes. Did she think I would know what was happening? Ma touched Philip. He looked up.

"I can't hear because there's a loud ringing."

"Back to bed," said Ma in a loud voice. "Your ears are tired." She helped him to his feet and put her arm around his shoulders.

The ringing in Philip's ears got so bad that after a few days Ma sent me to fetch Dr. Moody, but there was nothing he could do, so we waited and watched. Over the next couple of weeks Philip got back his appetite and his energy. At the same time it got harder to get his attention.

"Cuss," he said to me one morning when we were lying in bed. "How come the rooster don't crow anymore?" Just then the rooster let out a long, noisy cock-a-doodle-do. I looked at Philip. He hadn't heard.

"Beats me," I said quietly. Philip didn't respond, but I saw his eyes fill with tears. He knew. I gave him a shove with my foot. "Get up," I said as loudly as I could without shouting. Philip looked at my face.

"The ringing drowns out everything," he said.

"You'll get over it," I said, and I jumped up to get dressed.

"What?"

"Get up," I said, motioning with my head. "We have work to do!" I grinned and messed up his hair as he crawled out of bed. Would he get over it? I didn't know.

Ma put Philip to work in the yard and in the barn, tending the calves, gathering eggs in the morning, hoeing weeds in the yard. It was good to see him up and at it and he seemed to be doing better, but Ma still didn't let him go back to school.

Philip's cheeks filled out and the spring sunshine put a new batch of freckles on his nose, but it was clear that he couldn't hear most sounds. Once again Dr. Moody came up the hill to our house.

"This happens sometimes," said Dr. Moody. "The infection settles in the inner ear and does some form of damage to the nerve."

It was after supper and I'd just come in from the garden. The look on Ma's face told me plenty—first, that it wasn't good news; and second, that she was having trouble following the doctor's explanation. I listened carefully so I could explain later in Croatian.

"You could take him to a specialist," said the doctor, "but I think the chances for improvement are slim, and I'm afraid the mining company won't pay for it." Dr. Moody's face was sad and tired, and he looked ten years older than when I'd first met him. I wondered how often he had to give people bad news. Probably every day.

Ma frowned. "Take him where?"

"To Seattle," said Dr. Moody. "To the university. I'm only a general physician, and I could be wrong. There are doctors who specialize in hearing disorders, but I think they'd tell you the same thing," he said. "And it would cost a great deal of money."

"I get money," said Ma.

He put a big hand on Ma's shoulder. "Try not to get your hopes up." His face said a whole lot more than his words.

Ma nodded and dabbed her eyes with the corner of her apron.

I looked at Philip, whose eyes were as big as saucers. I crossed to where he was sitting and gave him a little shove. I motioned for him to follow me. "Come on," I said, making sure he could see my face. "Let's go feed the calves." He must have understood because he hopped off the stool and followed me out the back door. "So long, Dr. Moody," I said. "And thanks for coming again." I wanted to talk to him, tell him I'd looked up all the parts of the ear in *Gray's Anatomy* and knew all the Latin names by heart.

"Come on, Phil," I said instead, and we headed out the back door.

"Cuss," said Philip, "I can't hear nothing but ringing. Does that make me deaf?"

I shrugged. *"You ain't deaf,"* I said, making sure he could see my face. *"Just hard of hearing."* He squinted while I talked, as though screwing up his face like that would help him hear. *"Like Uncle Louie,"* I said.

Uncle Louie was a shot lighter. Over the years he'd grown deaf from all the dynamite blasts he'd lit, but it hadn't stopped him from working. Shot lighters made good money, and they didn't need to hear. They just needed to know how to set a charge, light a fuse, and run like the devil.

"Then maybe someday I'll get to be a shot lighter, too," said Philip.

"Maybe," I said.

I busied myself with milking, not wanting to look at my brother. What would become of a little squirt who couldn't hear? One thing was for sure—if he couldn't hear, he wouldn't finish grade two, or any other grade, for that matter.

We milked the cows and took the buckets to the calves. One by one I straddled them and held their heads while Philip held the buckets of milk. He'd named all of the calves. The heifer was Betsy, and the two bull calves were Billy and Jake. I concentrated on holding them while they ate so they wouldn't spill the milk. Soon they'd drink from the bucket without fighting so much, but they were still young, so it was easier if two people worked as a team.

In a short time Ma would sell Billy and Jake to Skinny's dad to be butchered for milk-fed veal, and that would mean cash. In two years Betsy would be grown and giving milk and then Ma would have four milk cows and a lot more milk to sell to neighbors. I hoped we could manage until then.

Chapter Twenty-Two

In late spring Ma sold the bull calves, Billy and Jake, to Mr. Giombetti for ten bucks apiece. She put the money in a strongbox under a kitchen floorboard. Whenever Matt and Joey sent us money, she put it in the strongbox, too. One day she announced that she was taking Philip to see a doctor in Seattle. The ringing had faded, but he still couldn't hear anything except the loudest noises. He hardly smiled and he didn't run or kick the ball around the yard. When his pal Pinky came by to play, Philip sat like a lump on the porch and didn't even want to shoot marbles.

"You haven't been on a train since you came to America, Ma," said Mary. "You sure you want to go?" Mary was visiting and we were eating supper. Ma had made a salad with the first lettuce from the garden.

I stuffed a forkful into my mouth and chewed. After months of beets and sauerkraut, the lettuce was as good as candy.

"I am taking Philip to Seattle tomorrow," said Ma in Croatian. "I don't know when we'll be back. Maybe a week, maybe more." That night she and Mary packed up and got ready for the trip.

I went to Mary and Hairy's for breakfast and supper every day while Ma and Philip were gone, but I stayed at our house at night. I'd never slept alone in the house before. The first night I lay awake, listening to every little sound. I lit the lamp and looked through Dr. Moody's big book until I was sleepy. After that, between schoolwork and the extra chores, by the time I climbed between the sheets, I was too bushed to fret.

One morning Skinny and I had just arrived at the schoolyard when I heard Perks's voice from behind us. "Hey! Boys!"

I hadn't seen my pal in weeks. It was great to lay eyes on him again. "What are you doing here?" I asked.

"How come you ain't at work?" asked Skinny.

"Got the day off," he said, but he didn't look happy about it. "I got something to tell you both."

"What is it?" asked Skinny.

Perks looked around. Then he opened his mouth to speak, but right then the principal rang the bell. "No time now," said Perks. "But come and see me later. It's big news. I'll be working at the cafe tonight, but I get a break to eat around eight."

"Yeah, hokey-dokey," said Skinny, hurrying into the school building without waiting for me. "'Bye, Perks."

"See you later," I said.

"Don't forget," said Perks.

"I won't."

Wondering about Perks's message was enough to keep me distracted from schoolwork all day. I figured Perks might be setting me and Skinny up for a prank. But maybe not. Maybe there was something important. One thing was for sure—I was curious.

When I got to the house after school, I was surprised to see Philip sitting on a stool drawing pictures with a pencil stub on a piece of brown wrapping paper.

"Hey! Squirt! How was the big city?" He didn't hear me. When I put my hand on his shoulder he jumped.

Ma already had on an apron and was busy at the stove. Her back was to me.

"Welcome home, Ma," I said. She turned around

and opened her arms for a hug. Her face looked old. "So how was Seattle?" I asked in Croatian, trying to sound cheerful.

"Too big," said Ma. "Lots of motor cars, lots of people, everything too expensive. The food was terrible. It rained every day." She turned back around and stirred what looked like beet soup.

Philip spoke. "We saw four doctors," he said.

"They didn't do a thing," said Ma.

"Rotten luck," I said.

"The doctors cost a bundle," said Philip.

I didn't ask how much.

"God will provide," said Ma. "I have the cows, the garden. I can wash clothes. And soon," she said, her back to Philip and me, "soon Slava can go to work. We will have all we need."

I patted Philip's shoulder and tried to smile. He hadn't heard any of what Ma'd said.

At supper Ma told me that she'd borrowed money against the house and now had six months to pay it back with interest, or the bank would foreclose.

"Three hundred bucks?" I said, dropping my spoon into the bowl of soup.

"I did what I did," said Ma.

"Couldn't you write to Matt?" I asked. Ma didn't answer at first. She took a sip of coffee.

"Slava, listen to me," she said. "Your brother Mate has a wife now, and a baby on the way. Soon Yosip will marry. They are in a good place, and I want them to be happy. They deserve their new life, Slava. My worries should not be theirs, not anymore. And besides, there are those bad men. Do you understand?"

"Yes." It wasn't just Joey and Matt Ma wanted to protect. It was Emmeline and Veronica and the baby that would soon be born.

Philip looked at Ma, then at me. His face was pale and he looked worried. We'd been speaking in Croatian. I doubted he'd understood much of it just from watching us.

"What's wrong?" Philip asked.

I reached over and messed up his hair. *"Nothing,"* I said, and put on a phony grin. I tweaked Philip's nose and he slapped at my hand. "School's out in a week," I said to Ma. "I'll start work right away." The words were out of my mouth before I could think twice. Ma nodded but didn't say a word. Philip finished his soup with a slurp.

"Good soup, Mama," he said.

I poked Philip in the arm to get his attention, made the squeezing gesture for milking, and the two of us got up to go take care of the animals.

Ma needed me. She needed my wages. Philip

needed my wages. My wages would mean the differ-
ence between keeping our house and losing it to the
bank. I was the oldest now. It was up to me to turn
our luck around. A full-time miner brought home a
hundred dollars a month. A boy had a duty to take
care of his mother. He didn't have to like it, he just
had to do it. I wondered if that was how Perks had
felt when his pa got burned.

Perks! I'd forgotten all about him. What could his
big news be? I finished my chores by eight and ran
down the hill to Skinny's house. He was waiting for
me outside the butcher shop. As soon as Skinny finished eighth grade, he'd be working full-time with
his pa. Perks was already working two jobs. Who was
I to think I could stay in school? My pals and I were
growing up and there was no way around it.

Chapter Twenty-Three

I knocked on the back door of the cafe and Perks himself answered. "Hey, boys," he said with a weary grin.

"What's up?" I said.

Perks's face turned serious and he nodded. He stepped outside and closed the door behind him.

"The mines are gonna start laying off," said Perks.

"That ain't a bit funny," said Skinny.

"Swear to God an' the Lord Jesus," said Perks. "Uncle Cedar heard it."

"They've been hiring all winter," I said, feeling like I'd been slapped. It couldn't be true. "I'm gonna quit school for good in June—to work."

Perks and Skinny stared at me.

"Liar," said Perks.

I shook my head. Saying it out loud felt worse than thinking it to myself.

"It's rotten luck for everybody," said Perks. "Coal orders are falling, and you know why? Fuel oil, that's why."

"Fuel oil?" said Skinny.

"That's right," said Perks. "Out east they're heating houses with oil. Uncle Cedar said there's even trains that run on oil now, instead of coal. And the mines are laying off, starting with everybody who ain't yet sixteen, such as yours truly." He paused to let that sink in. "All us boys," said Perks, "we're against the law to start with. And after that, all the coloreds, no matter how old, and then all the bachelors."

"How come you know this? Are you positive?" I asked. I had an itchy feeling that Perks knew what he was talking about.

"It ain't a rumor, if that's what you mean. It's a fact."

"They'll strike," said Skinny. "The miners'll strike."

"They won't strike," said Perks. "If the miners strike, the mines'll just shut down and that'll save them money, now, won't it? It's coming on summer-time anyhow. Coal orders is always down in summer. The miners that don't get laid off ain't gonna risk

160

getting fired, because if orders pick up, maybe they'll get hired on again."

Perks was right. I stared across the street at a couple walking arm in arm. Skinny swore. "When the mines lay off, Pop is real hard to live with." I eyed my tubby pal. His pa's temper was no secret.

"When's it starting?" I asked Perks.

"Anytime now."

"What are you gonna do?" I asked.

"I gotta work someplace," said Perks. "Ain't no choice. I'll figure out something." He didn't sound hopeful. "Helping at the cafe ain't enough. It don't bring in any actual cash."

Suddenly I had to get away, to be by myself and think this news through. "I have to go home," I said. "I'll see you two later." I didn't wait for either of them to say so long. I ran up the long hill to our house. Did Ma know? My head was as full as a potato bin in October. Perks was telling the truth. This was no trick or joke.

Ma was in the rocking chair, sewing a patch on one of Philip's shirts.

"The mines are laying off, Ma," I said. "Youngest first. There won't be any new hires." Ma put down her sewing and sighed.

"Take the heifer to Giombetti's," she said. "Go now, before I change my mind. I can't afford to feed a calf."

Philip looked from me to Ma and back again. I turned and went out to the barn. Philip followed close on my heels. "What are you doing, Cuss?"

Betsy came when I whistled, thinking she was going to get fed, but what she got was a rope around her neck and a walk down the hill.

"You ain't taking her to the butcher, are you, Cuss?" I didn't look at Philip. "She's gonna be a milk cow someday." I walked fast, ignoring my little brother's words. "Don't take her!" he yelled after me. "Don't take Betsy!"

Skinny's pop frowned when he saw the calf. "The meat, it ain't so good. This one been eating grass already, no?"

I nodded.

"I give you nine dollar."

"Thanks," I said.

When I got home, Ma put the money in the strongbox. I looked into the box before she closed it. Nine dollars was all we had.

When I got to school the next morning, Skinny was waiting in the yard.

"Did you hear?" he asked. "They laid off everybody sixteen and under. Every one of them," said Skinny. "Just last fall they couldn't wait to hire any old Joe with a pair of arms. Now this. Who'll buy meat when there's no money? Pop says if it lasts, we'll have to pack up and leave."

"And go where?" I asked.

Skinny shrugged. "Who knows. Maybe Seattle. Any place is better than Roslyn."

The schoolyard was buzzing with the news of the layoffs. Almost every kid in my class had a brother or cousin or uncle who'd been let go. It made the whole day gloomy despite the perfect June weather. Skunky must have known we were upset. She didn't drill us as hard as she had the week before. Exams were right around the corner, but our minds were far from school.

The town was turned upside down with the bad news. There were fistfights every night, and Dr. Moody stitched up more miners than ever before. There was talk that some of the local bootleggers were demanding immediate payments of debts. The saloons stopped selling drinks on credit. Folks looked grim, and groups of laid-off miners hung around downtown with nothing to do, waiting and wondering when the mines would rehire.

Aunts came by to cry and worry with Ma. Eight of my cousins and one uncle had been laid off.

Every day after school I worked in the garden or in the barn until supper, then I did my evening chores and spent the rest of the night studying for final exams. Matt and Joey sent a few dollars.

The end of seventh grade was only days away. I'd read all the short stories and knew them practically by heart. I'd memorized my Latin lessons. I'd worked arithmetic problems until I saw numbers in my sleep. I didn't have time to wonder where I'd find work once school let out, and I didn't have time to worry.

Finally the day for our school exams arrived. I'd studied so hard that my head hurt with all the facts. We took tests all morning. At lunchtime kids compared answers and tried to figure out their marks so far.

"I got the whole section on fractions wrong," said Skinny. "Who cares anyhow?"

"You should care," I said. "If you're going to run a butcher shop someday, you have to know all the particulars."

"All a butcher has to know is pounds and ounces, dollars and cents," said Skinny, "and how to divide a big cut of meat." He looked toward the school building. "Another three hours of tests. Yikes! I'm so nervous I have to pee the whole time. The Latin exam is going to kill me—I just know it."

"I studied till midnight," I said.

Skinny rolled his eyes. "Sometimes I think you got water for brains, Cuss. I wouldn't study if I knew I was never coming back to school. I'd go fishing. One more year—that's all I have."

The bell rang and we filed back into the building. Skunky made us sing all four stanzas of "My Country 'Tis of Thee" in order to digest our lunches better and get oxygen to our brains for the final set of exams.

Geography was first. Father Duval showed up ten minutes before we were done. He grinned and nodded as he watched us work, wiggling his bushy eyebrows in greeting and winking at kids who looked worried. At one-thirty Skunky asked us to put down our pencils and hand in our papers. She erased the geography test from the blackboard, and Father Duval began to write the Latin test. More than one kid groaned out loud.

"Class," said Father Duval as he wrote, "you are my star pupils, the best Latin students I have ever had. What a delight you have been! Such scholars." The truth was, except for a couple of us, most of the kids were rotten at Latin. "Please take out a sheet of clean paper," said Father Duval.

"Conjugate the following verbs"—he pointed at a list of ten verbs—"and then translate these sentences from English to Latin, and these phrases from Latin to English. What could be simpler? And for the very ambitious, when you are all finished with the test— and it is a simple one, no?—for ten extra points you may write one paragraph in Latin on the subject of your choice."

A quick look at the test told me I knew all the verbs. A baby could have conjugated that list. *Ire, edere, currere, orare, cantare, dicere, cupere, sequi, gustare, cogitare. Go, eat, run, pray, sing, speak, want, follow, taste, think.*

I stifled a grin. I didn't want to look like I'd just hit a home run when everyone else was down in the dumps. The first list of sentences was easy. I didn't have to think twice.

My dog eats bones. *Canis mea ossa edit.*
I have a younger sister. *Minor soror mihi est.*
My mother and father are kind. *Mater mea et
     pater meus sunt comites.*
I am thirteen years old. *Tredecim annos habeo.*
How old are you? *Quanti anni tibi habes?*
How do you do? *Quid agis?*
God is love. *Deus caritas est.*
Where is the meat market? *Ubi est carnis
     macellum?*
Have you ever been to England? *Fecistine iter
     ad Britanniam?*
The moon and the stars light the night sky.
     Luna et stellae noctis caelum illustrant.

The Latin sentences were a snap, too. I hadn't studied for nothing. I copied them down and wrote my answers beside them.

Ignoscere divinum est. To forgive is divine.
Vidistine calceos meos? Have you seen my shoes?
Quis est via Romam? Which is the road to Rome?
Pater meus senator est. My father is a senator.
Equi celeriter currunt. Horses run fast.
Amasne curricula? Do you like the races?
Milites proelio victi sunt. The soldiers lost the battle.
Aliquid carnis ede. Eat some meat.
Tres pueri natabant. Three boys went swimming.
Finis. The end.

That was it. I'd finished in just under an hour and hadn't lost a drop of sweat. I double-checked my answers. Every one was correct; I felt sure of it. I looked around at the other kids. They were biting their pencils and scratching their heads, but here I was with an hour to spare. I tore a fresh sheet of paper out of my school tablet. I didn't need any extra points, but writing a paragraph would kill time, so why not? This was my last chance to show off what I'd learned.

Father Duval asked us to hand in our exams just as I wrote the final sentence. Fact was, my essay had turned into two paragraphs. I hoped he wouldn't mind. Father Duval smiled and winked when I handed him my paper. I smiled back, partly because I was so darned proud of myself, and partly to hide how I really felt about handing in the last exam of my life.

The final bell rang and we left the building like a stampede of wild elephants. Most of the boys whooped and hollered on their way down the stairs. I suppose for a lot of them, getting out of school was like getting out of the slammer. Even though I knew I'd done well on the Latin test, I didn't feel like celebrating.

"How'd you do?" asked Skinny.

"Thumbs-up," I said, swallowing the lump in my throat so I wouldn't act like a girl in front of everyone.

"I did rotten," said Skinny. "Those exams were harder than I thought they'd be. The geography test was a doozy, but I think I passed. Oh, well. It's over now. Yahoo!" He twirled around and threw his cap in the air. I caught it and slapped it back on his head.

"Now what, Cuss?" asked Skinny, huffing to keep up with me as I hurried toward home.

"I gotta find work," I said.

"That's gonna be a trick," said Skinny.

I picked up my pace, wishing that my pal would let me be. Even if the mines weren't hiring, there had to be something. Skinny didn't understand going hungry or having a mortgaged house or watching your mother worry about money, and I sure wasn't about to explain it to him.

When we got to the butcher shop, I said, "See you later." Then I headed up the hill to my house. Perks was waiting for me there.

"What gives?" I asked.

Perks showed me a one-quart jar. "Ma sent me for some cream," said Perks. "For the cafe, but your ma didn't have any left. Since they gave me the boot at the Number Five, Ma's got me working at the cafe from breakfast until closing. Except for when I sneak off and get a little break before the next rush, like right now."

"School's out," I said, changing the subject. "I'm pretty sure I got good marks."

"What're you gonna do now that you ain't a schoolboy?"

"Work," I said. "Maybe my brother-in-law can get me something. He's a boss at the Number Five."

"I ain't counting on getting rehired," said Perks.

"I've been trying to find other work, but I ain't had no luck."

"You'll find something," I said, but I wasn't as sure as I sounded. It was always harder for the colored fellows to get jobs. Everyone knew it.

"Remember when we was little squirts, how we'd all go swimming at the hole soon as school was out?" said Perks. I nodded. "Looks like them times are over."

"Looks like," I said. "Tell your ma I'll bring her some cream first thing tomorrow morning."

"Thanks, pal," said Perks. He saluted, then headed down the hill.

My boots felt heavier than usual. No more exams. No more studying. No more sore behind from sitting all day on a wooden seat. No more fooling around all summer at the swimming hole. From here on out I was a wage earner. Goodbye, schoolboy; hello, working man.

After supper and chores, I wrapped Dr. Moody's anatomy book in brown paper and tied it with a string. I walked to his house. It was in Brookside neighborhood. I'd only been to his house in emergencies and hadn't really looked at it. The sign on the porch said D. MOODY, M.D.—COMPANY DOCTOR.

I knocked on the door. Dr. Moody's pretty wife

answered the door. She had a red-haired baby on her hip. "Yes?"

"Hello, ma'am," I said, whipping off my cap. "I'm returning a book that Dr. Moody loaned me a while back."

"You must be Cuss," she said. "The boy who"— she grinned—"knows a lot of languages." I felt my face turn red. "Donald told me all about you. I'll tell him you're here. He's in the office, in back."

I shook my head. "No," I said, "don't bother him. I'll just put this down here because it's really heavy." I placed the book on a chair by the door. "And please tell him I said thanks."

"I hope it was helpful," said Mrs. Moody. The baby pulled her hair. "No, no, Melvin," she said to the baby, untangling his fingers from her hair.

"It was very helpful," I said. "Thanks."

I walked down the steps. I didn't need books anymore. What I needed was a job.

Chapter Twenty-Four

The next day I went looking for work. I stopped in at every store in town. Mr. Forelli paid me a nickel to unload ten fifty-pound flour sacks from a wagon and carry them down to the bakery cellar. That night after the quitting whistle blew, the town was buzzing with the news that more men had been laid off.

The next morning the stable boy didn't show up at the company store, so I fed and watered the big horses, hitched them to the delivery wagon, and shoveled out the stalls. That earned me twenty-five cents. Ma let me keep a penny of it. I asked the stable boss if he needed me the next day, but by then word had gotten out about the stable boy not showing up and there were four grown men asking for the job.

Two weeks after school let out, I picked up my report card at the school office. I got an A-plus in Latin and an A in every other subject. When I showed the report card to Ma, she hugged me and said she was proud. Then she asked me to deliver a quart of cream to the Pavankas. I brought back the nickel and she tucked it into her apron pocket.

Every time I heard about a job, so did every other fellow in town. For the rest of June I brought in a grand total of fifty-five cents to the family coffers. If I'd been a girl, I could have gotten girls' work, like ironing or doing wash, but instead I had to try to get the same jobs that all the other fellows in Roslyn were after.

We got two letters from Matt on the last day of June, one for Ma and one for me. Emmeline's little brother, Hughie, delivered them to Ma folded up inside a lace tablecloth that needed mending. When Ma handed me the letter with my name on it, I had to stifle the urge to jump up and down and shout. There wasn't any stamp, and no postmark, so I figured it must have come inside the letter for Ma. I wanted to rip open the letter right then and there, but instead I put it in my pocket to save for later.

The big news in Ma's letter was a twenty-dollar bill, a five, and two ones. Twenty-seven bucks! Matt and Joey had been putting in some overtime.

After evening chores I climbed up into the hay-loft and read my letter.

Heydee-ho, Cuss!

How's things in my old digs? Did you pass all
your exams? With flying colors, I bet. You've got
a brain between your ears, li'l bro. Best to put it to
good use. None of that pickax swinging for you,
eh, what? You make me proud. Someday folks
will call you "Mister." I'm warning you right now,
I've heard from certain quarters that grade eight
is not a piece of cake. Get ready to put your nose
to the grindstone. Don't lose any brain cells over
the summer.

Emmeline is front-heavy, but she's still the
prettiest wife around. Joey says howdy. His gal is
a real sweetheart. Speaks Spanish. I'm sure she
could teach you a word or two, but then, she's a
lady, so maybe not. Ha-ha!

I hope you have a dandy time swimming and
fishing and cutting up this summer. Stay out of
trouble, don't eat too many grapes, and keep your
eye on baby Phil.

Yours truly,
Matt

I stared at the paper. I read the words three times.

Matt and Joey didn't know Philip had been sick. They didn't know he was as deaf as a post and that Ma had spent every red cent on doctors and that the brood sows had kicked the bucket. They didn't know the house had a mortgage. They didn't know the mines were laying off. They thought life was peachy and that Ma was getting by on her pension, the milk she sold, odd jobs, and the money they sent. They didn't know any of the truth.

Matt and Joey wouldn't want Ma to lose the house. My belly growled. We weren't out of food yet, but there wasn't any extra and I never got enough to fill me. Matt would want to know that.

There was a roar of drunken laughter downtown. I thought about the night Simms died, and it turned my empty belly over with a big flop. I knew why Ma hadn't let them know the score, why she didn't dare write to them. Ma was still worried about the mobsters.

But maybe she didn't need to worry anymore. Nearly ten months had passed. Maybe Ma was being too careful. I read Matt's letter again and again, until there wasn't enough light in the barn to see the words.

Chapter Twenty-Five

Two nights later Leroy Kepke and Charliehorse Bodoni were dead, knifed in the woods behind the Number Seven. No one saw or heard a thing. As usual there were plenty of rumors. I ran into Perks the afternoon after it had happened. I was bringing Geraldine down from the hills.

"Bootleg killing," said Perks. He was on his way to find their cow, Jezebel. "Lotta folks are saying it smells like a Mob hit."

"Says you," I said, peeved that Perks always had the inside story. "Roslyn is a backwater. The mobsters wouldn't bother."

"Says you, Cuss. There's people who know," said Perks. "And I heard it from them, so it's as reliable as the sun comes up. I can't tell you who."

"They could have been fighting over a gal," I said. "No one knows what happened."

"It wasn't no accident," said Perks. "And they didn't kill each other. That's certain."

"You don't know," I said.

"Yeah, well, it's a good thing your brothers got out when they did, and that's all I got to say on the matter."

Perks could be wrong about the bootlegger business, but it wasn't likely. Somewhere in Roslyn, or maybe in a nearby town, a murderer walked free. Two more fellows were dead. And all because of whiskey.

For supper that night we had beet soup and plain bread, no butter. The coffee was watery and bitter. Even though I was starved, nothing tasted good. I couldn't stop thinking about the two dead men.

Someone knocked at the front door. Ma answered it, and as soon as we saw who it was, Philip and I were on our feet.

"*Hvaljen Isus i Marija*," said Father Duval. *Praised be Jesus and Mary.* He had his hat in his hand and a great smile on his face. Hearing the badly pronounced Croatian greeting coming from the French priest made me want to laugh. Instead, I made the proper response with Ma.

"*Vazda hvaljen*," we answered in Croatian. *Forever praise.*

"What did you say?" asked Philip.

"Better than the first time, eh, Slava?" said Father Duval.

I felt my face turn red. I was still ashamed of myself for correcting a priest, even if he did flub. "Perfect, Father," I said.

"Good, good."

"Come in," said Ma. Her voice was nervous. A priest in your house was a big deal for an Old Country person. Last time he'd been here it was on account of Philip. She'd been too upset to be nervous then. "You like beet soup, eh, Father?"

"Oh, no, I have had my supper already. I can't stay but a minute. I am wondering if Slava can help me tomorrow."

"Yes," said Ma without even so much as a glance in my direction. "Anything Father need, Slava do. He is smart, good boy."

"A fine Latin scholar, indeed," said Father Duval. "But what I need is one more altar boy for the funerals," he said. "I hate for it to be one of the smaller boys for these funerals." His grin had melted away and his face was sad. It hadn't occurred to me until right then that even though priests buried people all the time, some funerals must be worse than others. "Young Joseph Giombetti suggested Slava."

"Yes, Slava can do," said Ma. Now her face was beaming. "He is best altar boy."

"I haven't done it for more than a year," I said. "And I don't have any shoes." I'd been an altar boy like every other boy, until I was old enough to get out of it.

Ma ignored me. "Slava help. What time?"

"The first funeral, Mr. Kepke, is at nine, and the second, Mr. Bodoni, at eleven."

"Good," said Ma. "Slava will go."

"Thank you," said Father Duval. *"Au revoir. Laku noć."* He bowed and left.

Ma closed the door behind him and fanned herself with her hand. "Imagine," she said in Croatian, "the priest dropping by our house like that. And now, Slava has work. Even if there's no money, it gives us riches in heaven." Ma sat back down at the table. Her cheeks were bright red and she looked pleased as punch. "When a priest comes to your house, it's practically like a blessing. Now finish up your supper."

Leave it to Skinny to volunteer me for altar-boy service at two funerals in one day. I finished my soup, and even though I wasn't full, I didn't ask for more.

That night I lay awake thinking about the funerals. Matt's old boots were too tight now, but they'd have to do. I hoped I'd remember how to do everything right. Skinny was an altar boy all the time. I'd have him give me a review of the Latin responses ahead of time. The thought of Skinny volunteering for funeral duty gave me a chuckle. Funerals were second only to weddings when it came to food. At least tomorrow my belly would be full.

The next morning just after breakfast, Ma handed me a package wrapped in paper and tied with string. I opened it up. Inside was a pair of old-fashioned shoes. They were shiny brown leather, with buttons, and they looked big enough to fit me.

"Your father's," said Ma. "He wore them to our wedding, and when we got off the ship in America." I ran my hands over the smooth toes. The heels were barely worn. "I should have buried him in them, but I had four sons . . . and he didn't need them anymore."

"They're swell, Ma," I said.

"You need them," said Ma, "to be an altar boy."

I'd never had a pair of real shoes. And I didn't have anything that had belonged to my pa. "I'll take good care of them," I said.

Ma nodded. "Mate and Yosip were in such a hurry to jump the train that I didn't have time to give them the shoes," said Ma, polishing one of Pa's shoes with her sleeve. "And when Emmeline left, I forgot because of Mary's wedding. So now they are your shoes." I felt my heart speed up. I bent over and held the shoes next to my bare feet. *Matt and Joey had jumped a train.* It was the first real information I'd had so far.

When I got to the church, Skinny gave me the lowdown on what to do and when. We put on our long white albs. Then I wiped my bare feet on a towel, pulled on a pair of wool socks, and put on Pa's fancy shoes. I didn't have a button hook, so it took a while. Skinny whistled when he noticed my shoes.

"My pop has a pair of those," he said. "Handmade in Italy."

We lit candles and got everything ready. I thought about my brothers jumping a train.

The funeral crowd was grim, and the weather didn't help any. The day started out dark and cloudy, and by the time Father Duval was incensing Leroy Kepke's casket, the rain was hammering on the church roof.

There was more crying than usual, some down-right sobbing out in the crowd. I concentrated on my duties and tried not to glance in that direction. I'd been to plenty of funerals. Who hadn't? Of course they were sad, but this one really got to me. I tripped on my alb when somebody wailed. A shiver raced up my backbone with cold bare feet. The poor sap in the coffin could have been one of my brothers.

It was all I could do to pay attention during the

mass. My brothers had left Roslyn so this wouldn't happen to them. They'd jumped a train. During one of the prayers, instead of wishing Leroy's soul a hop and a skip through purgatory, I thanked God that Joey and Matt had gotten clean away. Ma was right to be tight-lipped.

The long procession wove through the streets of the town and up to the graveyard. Leroy Kepke was given back to the earth on a drizzly day in early July. When we were finished, Father Duval and Skinny and I headed back to church for Charliehorse's funeral.

It could have been Joey. It could have been Matt. For the first time since that bad night almost a year ago, I knew for certain that they could never come back to Roslyn.

There were mountains of food at the funeral lunch. Skinny and I chowed down until I felt as fat as he looked.

"Any luck finding work?" asked Skinny with his mouth full of spice cake.

"Nothing," I said.

"Too bad," said Skinny. "Business is down for Pop, too. Lotta people are leaving. It's changing the town."

"Any more talk about leaving town?"

"Nah, Ma said it was just crazy talk. Pop drank a lot of wine that night." Probably wine made from last year's grapes, I thought. I watched Skinny bite into another piece of cake. Would we have to leave town, too? Sometimes folks went back to the Old Country. Would we? What would happen if Ma lost the house?

I hated not knowing what was going to happen next, and I wished Ma would fill me in with some details. I wasn't a little punk who couldn't take it. Matt had called me the man of the house, but Ma still treated me like a kid, even if I did fit Pa's shoes. I picked a slice of cold sausage off my plate and stuck it in my mouth.

"That's one of our pepperonis," said Skinny. "Pop's secret recipe."

I hadn't eaten anything this good in months. No wonder Skinny was so fat. He got pepperoni anytime he wanted, while we lived on soup. We needed money. And we needed it soon.

"Your pa doesn't need another assistant, does he?" I asked.

Skinny laughed. "Are you kidding? He's got Luigi already, and me and Helen work for free."

I lowered my voice. "Do you think anyone else will get it?"

Skinny's dark brown eyes got huge. "There's talk," he said, "but who knows? Pop says the town is falling apart at the seams."

He picked up a third piece of cake and started to eat it. I found a raisin bun and bit into it. We ate desserts until the ladies started cleaning up the parish hall. On our way out the door, Father Duval called to me.

"Slava, please wait," he said.

Skinny waved and headed home. My belly was full to bursting, and so was my brain. An idea was beginning to cook, helped no doubt by all the rich food.

Father Duval came over and put a hand on my shoulder. "I need a favor." I nodded. Father Duval leaned in close and lowered his voice. "The good parish ladies, they give me the leftover food." He swept his hand around at the tables where the women were gathering up the leftovers into piles of meats, breads, and sweets. "Every funeral, every wedding, it is the same," he whispered. "See how fat I am?"

I wasn't about to agree with him. I kept my mouth shut and tried not to smile.

"I need you to come back later, take some of this food away." The look on his face was desperate. Probably because he was French. Everyone knew Frenchies were emotional, almost as bad as wops.

"But it's for you, Father," I protested, eyeing a pile of sliced porketta half as high as a milk pail. "It wouldn't be right."

"It would be a sin for a fat man such as myself to eat that food," said Father Duval. "It would be gluttony! And it would also be a sin to throw away so much food, but if I try to give it back to the ladies, they are insulted, and—poof!—I have sinned again by insulting my parishioners with my ungratefulness." I nodded. Father Duval was clearly in a moral pickle. "So you come back after the ladies have cleaned up, take some of this food off my hands, and I would be so grateful. You would be helping to make this sinner into a holy priest."

"Hokey-dokey," I said. Father Duval patted me on the back.

"I need an altar boy for the Pasquan wedding on Saturday. Would you mind?"

"Not a bit," I said.

"*Hvala,*" he said in Croatian. *Thank you.*

I told him I'd be back in about an hour.

"Bring two milk pails," said Father Duval, "at the least."

An hour later I was heading home with two buckets filled to the brim with meats and sweets. Father Duval had kept the bread. "It is really all I should eat," he'd said. "Bread and water, after all of that funeral food in one day. It is my penance."

Ma was none too pleased. "No charity," she said in English.

"It's a favor," I explained, "for the priest." I switched to Croatian to get the point across. "Father begged me to take it so he would avoid the sin of gluttony. It was my Christian duty."

Ma thought about it a minute and then nodded. "He is a holy priest," she said finally. "Too bad he's French."

I did my evening chores with a full stomach for the first time in weeks. Before all the troubles had started, we'd always had enough to eat. I was tired of going hungry. I made sure Philip took extra pepperoni at supper.

Funeral food was nice, but by hook or by crook, I had to get my hands on some money. I was starting to think I might know how.

Chapter Twenty-Six

That night I read my poetry book to keep from falling asleep. I read a story poem about an Indian water boy named Gunga Din. At first it was exciting, and then it was sort of sad, but I liked it anyway.

When I was sure Ma had gone to bed, and the downtown crowd was starting to liven up, I sneaked out and went down the hill. I headed north to the colored part of town. The rain had stopped and the air was damp. The bars were alive with men, drinking and playing cards and forgetting the fact that jobs were drying up like a puddle in August. Somewhere, maybe right here in Roslyn, Leroy and Charliehorse's killer was hanging out, yukking it up with the rest of the miners. I hurried as I went and kept clear of the saloons.

I got to the colored cafe and knocked. Perks answered and his face broke into a dandy grin. "Hey, Cuss, old pal," he said, wiping his wet hands on his apron. "Come on in."

I stepped into the back room off the kitchen. Someone was singing out in the main room. Other people were laughing. Perks's little sister Eunice came in with a tray under one arm.

"I'm telling Ma you ain't working," she said.

"Skedaddle, pea brain," said Perks. Eunice stuck out her tongue, filled the tray with clean glasses, and carried it back out into the dining room.

"I gotta talk to you," I said. "It's important."

Someone hollered out, "Two fried ham sandwiches, double onions!"

"Got it!" yelled another voice, which I recognized as Perks's ma.

"Talk fast," said Perks. "We're real busy."

"I want to go find my brothers," I said, "and work cutting trees. You could come with me." I let the idea sink in, watching Perks's face in the pale light of the electric bulb.

"You have to be eighteen to cut trees," said Perks.

"Matt said they were earning overtime," I said. "That means the lumber company doesn't have enough workers. If they need arms and legs, they'll take us."

"So where are your brothers?" asked Perks. "Did you find out?"

"My ma said they hopped a train, and if they're west of the mountains, it must've been a freighter to Seattle."

"You gonna hop a train?" said Perks.

I nodded. "We can ask around, find out where the lumber camps are," I said. "I'll find my brothers and hook up with them and send all the money I earn home. I can't earn a nickel in this town."

"Ma would kill me," said Perks.

"Send her a fat stack of lumberjack wages and you'll be her darlin' baby boy forever." I crossed my fingers hard and kept talking. I didn't want to carry out my scheme alone. "My ma would kill me, too, if she knew. But it ain't like running away—not if I go to my brothers."

"They ain't *my* brothers," said Perks.

"Don't matter," I said. "Matt and Joey'll help you. You know it, too." I saw Perks nod.

"Yeah, they're square."

"The point is, get work, send home the cash, and all will be forgiven," I said. And Ma wouldn't lose the house and everything else. I didn't tell him that part. Perks scratched his chin.

"I can swing an ax good as anyone."

"Me, too," I said.

"So, when do we go?" asked Perks. He held out his hand and we shook on the deal.

"Soon as we figure out the train situation," I said. "Ask around, Perks. See if anyone knows where the lumber camps are. We need to find out exactly where to get off the train."

"Don't your brothers write?" I nodded. "Then there has to be a mark on the letters, from the town where they're mailed from."

"I've never seen any envelope," I said, "just the letters. I don't know where they come from."

"Your brothers is hiding out from the big-city bootleggers, so it ain't likely they'll be easy to find," said Perks. "Maybe they don't even use their own names now." He snapped a fly with his dish towel. It fell to the floor. I thought of Leroy and Charliehorse, and a cold shiver crawled up my back.

A woman's voice yelled out, "Percy! I need clean plates!"

"Back to my sink for now," said Perks. "I'll work on the situation."

We had a plan. Perks was in with me. I ran all the way home.

I fell asleep counting out imaginary silver dollars to give to Ma. She'd be ticked at me for running off to work, but she'd forgive me when she had a load of hard-earned moolah in her hands, enough to pay off the mortgage. I wasn't going to stick around and watch her lose the house. Philip could take care of all the chores. Ma didn't need me here. She needed me to earn money, and fast. I was getting out of Roslyn to do just that.

I woke up three hours later. It was Philip's birthday, so I woke him with a tweak on the nose and eight swats on his little rump. I told him I'd do his milking. I hummed "Yankee Doodle Dandy" while I did the morning chores, and I gave Ma a big hug when I came into the house for breakfast.

"The polenta smells divine," I said.

"Filip's favorite breakfast," said Ma. "Sit. Eat." She grinned and waved her spoon at me. I wished I could tell her my plan, but my lips were sealed. Our luck was about to take a turn for the better.

Chapter Twenty-Seven

The next day while Ma was delivering clean laundry, I lifted up the floorboard in the kitchen and looked in the strongbox. It wasn't like looking was a sin, I told myself, feeling like a regular hoodlum. I wasn't stealing, just snooping, checking to see if there were any envelopes with a postmark. My heart beat so hard that I thought for sure someone would hear it. There was no sign of Matt's letters. There wasn't any money, either. Not even two bits. Our baptismal certificates were there, Ma and Pa's immigration papers, Pa's death certificate, and a paper from the bank. It was written in highfalutin lawyer language, but I understood the gist, partly because of all the Latin I'd learned. Ma had to pay back her loan by December 30, 1926, or the bank would take possession of the property. I didn't know how much she'd paid back already, but it probably wasn't much to sneeze at.

For the next few days I puzzled over how to get the information I needed. I worked in the garden, mended the fence, picked caterpillars off the fruit trees, and mucked out the barn. While I worked, I memorized the first part of a long poem called *The Rime of the Ancient Mariner,* right up to the part where the sailor shot the albatross with his crossbow. Father Duval sent word that he needed an altar boy for two more funerals, a day apart. I didn't have to ask Ma for permission. And this time I didn't expect her to complain about the food I brought home.

Both of the funerals were for old folks, nothing like when Leroy and Charliehorse had died. Skinny and I gorged ourselves.

Sunday afternoon I took Philip down to the river. It was a hot day but the water was ice-cold. I'd just pulled myself out onto the bank and felt the goose bumps prickling my back when I saw Perks running down the hill toward us.

"Hey!" he said. He was out of breath. "I went to your house and your ma said you were at the swimming hole." He glanced over at Philip, who was sitting about four feet away. I shook my head at Perks to let him know Philip wouldn't hear a thing.

"What?" I asked.

"I got some news from Uncle Cedar's pal Banjo, the one who plays in the colored band. Banjo does odd jobs for the railroad, and he was up real early one morning, on account of there was a bad tie and the train couldn't go nowhere until it was fixed. Anyhow, Banjo seen your brothers. One of them had a guitar. That's how he knew it was Matt."

"What did you find out?"

"You ain't gonna believe it, Cuss." He paused, and I wanted to shake him to make him hurry up.

"So give over," I said.

"I know where your brothers is." Perks grinned. He was enjoying making me wait. "It took some doing. I had to pull Banjo a free bucket of beer, but Mama wasn't looking at the time."

"Liar," I said.

"Swear to God," he said. "This is the gospel truth."

"So where?" I glanced around. No one was listening. Perks leaned close.

"California."

My mouth dropped open and I gaped at Perks like an idiot. When I could finally talk, all I said was, "Liar."

"How many times do I gotta swear to God before you believe me?" asked Perks. "It's true. True as this river is full of water."

"They're cutting trees in California?" I asked. I hardly heard my own words. How had my brothers gotten to California? It was a thousand miles away.

"Banjo didn't say nothing about what kind of work. He only said he seen them," said Perks.

"How'd they get to California?" I asked, and as soon as the words were out of my mouth, I knew. Perks grinned as I said, "The grape train?"

"The one and only," said Perks. "Guess it didn't leave as empty as everybody thought."

A crow sailed overhead. Philip threw a pinecone into the water. I watched as it floated downstream. All my plans disappeared like dandelion fluff in the wind. I bit my lower lip to keep it still.

"It's always sunny in California," said Perks. "And there's orange trees everywhere. And jobs. That's what Banjo says."

Ma had kept her secret, all right. Angry tears welled up in my eyes, but I blinked them away. So what if there were jobs? We'd never find my brothers now.

"Once Ma told me if she had two hundred bucks cash she could buy the cafe," said Perks. "Nobody in our family ever owned a thing. I'm gonna earn her that two hundred. I'm going to California!" I stared at his face. Perks's dark eyes twinkled like the devil's own.

"But it's a thousand miles away," I said. "It ain't

like hopping the train to Seattle." The trip to Seattle would have taken only hours. Who knew how long it would take to get to California?

"Skinny says the grape train's coming in two weeks, more or less," said Perks. "He got it from Helen, who had to wash up all the wine bottles."

"I don't know, Perks," I said.

"Cuss, this is better than going west of the mountains," said Perks. "Ma has a second cousin once removed who's in California. Bobby Jester, that's his name. He works for the railroad, serving on one of them fancy Pullmans. Now, that's a job! White gloves and everything. There's work. We just have to get ourselves down there."

"White boys don't work in Pullmans," I said.

"It's just a for-instance," said Perks. "We could prospect for gold, like the forty-niners."

"Now you're talking like a bonehead," I said.

"I figure you oughta be able to rustle up some information on where your brothers are working. And maybe they ain't cutting trees. Who knows? It's the Golden State, Cuss. They could be doin' anything."

"I don't know where Matt and Joey ended up," I said. "That's the problem. I thought they were near Seattle someplace. California is a whole state, and a big one to boot, twice as big as Washington."

"Do everything you can to find out," said Perks. "We gotta know beforehand, or we can't even start."

I nodded. We needed facts. How long would it take to get there? What kind of work were they doing? Were there lumber camps in California? I didn't know. Now that I knew part of the story, how could I get the rest?

"Does Banjo know where in California the grape train goes?" I asked.

Perks shrugged. "Beats me, but a free bucket of beer might help him recollect."

"And even if we do find out where it goes, how do we know where Joey and Matt got off?" I was talking to myself as much as to Perks. "Hopping the train to Seattle is like a stroll to the outhouse compared to this," I said. "I just don't know. I want to think about it some."

"You chicken?" asked Perks.

"No," I said, but it was a lie, pure and simple.

"Well, it's a good thing, 'cause you and me need to apply all our brainpower to the situation or we'll never get out of this coal town. This is our big chance. Two weeks, maybe less, and the grape train chugs into Roslyn loaded with fruit. If we ain't on that train when it turns around and goes back to California, there's no way we find your brothers, no way we send no cash to nobody back home." A note of pleading had crept into Perks's voice. "My pa ain't never gonna work again, Cuss. I gotta go."

I took a deep breath. "Hokey-dokey," I said. I picked up a pinecone and threw it into the river. Philip saw it go in and looked up, surprised. So many things surprised him. I wondered what it was like to be deaf. What went on in his head now that he couldn't hear the rest of the world happening around him? "I'll find out what I can, Perks," I said. "You work on Banjo." I watched as Philip tossed a stick into the current.

If I sent enough money home, maybe Ma would find a doctor who could fix Phil's ears. My heart beat a little faster and I felt my lips curl up into a grin. I had to get to California. It was the only way.

Chapter Twenty-Eight

Finding out where the grape train came from turned out to be a cakewalk. On Saturday Father Duval asked Skinny and me to be altar boys for a wedding. We were stuffing our faces afterward when Skinny brought up the subject.

"Hey, the grape train's coming in a couple of weeks," said Skinny.

"I know," I said, chewing an especially juicy piece of sausage. "Perks told me."

"Yeah, well, you got a plan for getting grapes?" Skinny smacked his lips and wiggled his eyebrows.

"Didn't you get your fill last year?" I asked.

"Not possible," said Skinny. "I have this idea." He looked around to see if anyone was listening. The band was getting ready to strike up another dance, and there were plenty of people laughing and talking. "I could tie a pillow to my head, in case you drop the box on my head again. Maybe a couple of pillows." He was dead serious and it made me laugh out loud.

"You need an army helmet, that's what," I said.

Skinny stuffed a thick slice of walnut povitica into his mouth, stood at attention, and saluted. I let him chew it and swallow. Before he got a chance to eat another thing, I popped the question. "Did you ever notice where that grape train comes from?" Skinny's best subject was geography. I crossed my fingers that the grape train had interested my chubby pal for more reasons than grapes.

"California, ya dummy," said Skinny. He reached for a raisin bun.

"I meant *where* in California. It's a big state."

"Place called Napa. I read it on the side of the boxcar when I was waiting for a certain pal of mine to drop a crate on my head. Napa, California. Sounds like a good place to take a snooze. Hey, maybe three pillows would work," he said, and bit the raisin bun in half.

On the short walk home, I made a list in my head of what I knew for sure. Joey and Matt had hopped the grape train. The grape train came from a place called Napa. Wherever my brothers ended up, they were making enough money to send some to Ma, at first anyhow, and to get married to boot. The grape train was coming to Roslyn soon. Perks and I had to be on that train when it left.

I needed one more piece of information. It turned out that I only had to wait two days to get it.

I got home and found a note on the kitchen table:

Mary's baby is coming.

"Cuss, we're gonna be uncles," said Philip, hopping up and down with excitement.

"You'll be a good uncle," I said, exaggerating my words so Phil could read my lips. If I took it slow, he could usually understand. I grabbed a clean milk pail out of the kitchen.

"I hope it's a boy," said Philip. "Do you like the name Robert?"

I shrugged. I didn't care what kind of baby it was, and I sure as heck didn't care what they named it. All I cared about was finding my big brothers. Time was running out.

"It's a good thing Mary married Hairy," said Philip. "Not that other guy."

While I milked I thought about how Mary had paid me to do her milking that night when everything had gone wrong. In some ways Mary was the whole reason Joey and Matt had had to leave and our luck had gone sour. Why'd she ever gotten mixed up with that Simms?

Did Mary know where Matt and Joey were?

My brain started to race and I hurried through the milking. Ma wouldn't tell me, but maybe Mary would. Why hadn't I thought of her before? She'd given me a poetry book, hadn't she? People didn't give poetry books to stupid little squirts. Maybe Mary would think I was old enough to be in on the family secret.

I knew I had a chance. And I knew I had to do it just right.

Ma came home after midnight. I elbowed Philip and he woke up. I pointed down the stairs and we pulled on our overalls and went down to the kitchen. Ma was stirring milk on the stove.

"The baby is a boy," she said in Croatian. "A fat, fine one. And Mary is feeling well. It was an easy first baby. Clement is so proud. I am a grandmother at last! Praised be Jesus and Mary." She dabbed at her eyes.

"A boy," I said to Philip, making sure he understood.

He grinned from ear to ear.

"What did they name him?" I asked, rubbing the sleep from my eyes and stifling a yawn.

"Walter," Ma meant to say, but it came out "Val-ter." Ma never could make the American W sound.

"What?" asked Philip, patting Ma on the arm to get her attention.

"Valter," said Ma slowly, looking right at Philip.

"I like Robert better," he said with a pout. "I don't think Valter is a saint name. I don't think Father Duval will baptize him if his name is Valter."

"It's *Walter,*" I said, emphasizing the W.

"Oh," said Philip. "That's better."

"Clement bought cocoa to make hot chocolate for a celebration," said Ma. "His mother made some for us and for Mary. She's a good woman," said Ma. "And his sisters are good, too. Good people. They sent home cocoa for all of us. Sugar, too."

Ma chattered about this and that, sometimes in English, mostly in Croatian, smiling and stirring and pouring cocoa for Philip and me.

I hadn't seen Ma so cheerful in weeks, and it got me to thinking. Plotting a getaway with Perks was exciting. It had taken up most of my time. Now I looked around and it seemed like leaving home would be about the stupidest thing I could ever do. I shoved the thought and the feeling that went with it right out of my brain.

"When can we see Walter?" I asked, testing my cocoa to make sure it wouldn't burn my tongue.

I'd only had cocoa once before, at a wedding in the middle of winter. I'd burned my tongue that time.

"Tomorrow," said Ma. "I'm sure Clement will want to show off his firstborn son. He's a big baby, with more hair than his father!" Ma chuckled at her own comment. How dandy to see her laughing and joking again. That was why I had to leave home and find a good job. I was doing it for Ma, so she could go back to being happy instead of weighed down by worries.

I made a joke in Croatian about Hairy's head looking like a boiled egg. Ma laughed hard. I explained to Philip what I'd said, and he laughed, too. It felt like we hadn't made any jokes in ages, not since Joey and Matt had gone away. Matt would love being an uncle. He'd probably write a funny song about it, too. I'd tell him about Walter and the hot cocoa when I got to California.

After I'd finished the last drop of cocoa and put the cup into the dishpan, I headed back to bed. *"Laku noć, baka,"* I said to Ma. *Good night, Grandmother.*

Ma grinned and bowed in my direction. *"Laku noć, ujo Slava,"* she said. *Good night, Uncle Slava.*

My feet felt heavier than usual on the stairs. I didn't have a choice. Seeing Ma so happy made me sure of my decision. No one suspected that I was getting ready to hightail it out of town. I knew Ma and

Philip would miss me. But on the other hand, I'd be one less mouth to feed.

I took off my overalls and slid between the sheets. After a while Philip came up, too, and crawled into bed with me. "Good night, Uncle Cuss," he said, and then he turned over and went right to sleep. For a few seconds, while we were lying there in the dark together, it almost felt like old times.

Chapter Twenty-Nine

When I knocked at Mary's door the next morning, Hairy's little sister, Estelle, opened it and invited me in. "I came to see the baby," I said, "and my sister." I'd brought a bucketful of ripe transparent apples, Mary's favorite. "These are for Hairy—I mean, Clement and Mary—from our tree," I said, handing the bucket to Estelle.

She took the apples and pointed upstairs. "She's up there. You can go up."

"Mary?" I hollered up the stairs.

"Come on up, Cuss," she said. She sounded like her normal self, not tired or sick. I wasn't sure what to expect, but, then, cows were normal after having a baby. Why not girls?

Mary was propped up in bed and little Walter was

feeding noisily at her breast. He sounded just like a piglet. "Walter is in the middle of breakfast," she said. "You can see his face in a minute." I smiled and looked away. I'd been around plenty of women who were feeding babies, but this was my sister. Having a baby made Mary a grown-up, and suddenly I felt shy.

"He's bald," I said stupidly.

Mary laughed and patted the baby's head. "No, he isn't," she said. "He's just fair. Look." She pulled up a few strands of soft blond hair, about an inch long. "Clement was towheaded as a baby," she said. I wanted to say "Back when he had hair," but I didn't. Instead, I told Mary about the apples.

"I brought you some transparent apples. They're really fine this year. Hardly any worms."

"Thanks," she said. "I planted a little tree outside in April, but it won't have apples for a few years." The baby squawked and fussed and Mary tended to him.

I fished around for something to say, anything other than what I'd practiced saying, what I'd really come for. The time wasn't right. Not yet. "When is he getting baptized?" I asked.

"This Sunday, of course," said Mary. "Petar and Jane will be the godparents." Jane was a cousin from Ma's side of the family. Mary didn't look up from her baby but stared at him as he settled back to eating.

"Philip was worried that Walter isn't a saint's name." Mary laughed, which startled Walter, who began to wail.

"Sorry, baby," she said. "Shh! Shh!" Walter settled down again. I still hadn't seen his face. "I don't know if Walter is a saint's name or not," said Mary. "Philip would worry. He's such a worrier, at least now." Her face got serious. She stroked Walter's little head. "Clement and I decided to give Walter two names. How does Walter Andrew sound? Andrew is a saint's name, same as Papa's, may he rest in peace." She crossed herself and so did I. Mary had memories of Pa. I only had shadows.

"What will he do when he gets confirmed?" I asked, thinking of the confirmation name I'd chosen for myself: Jerome.

"I guess he'll have three names then," said Mary. "All the young couples are giving their babies a middle name now when they're born."

"I don't guess it matters how many names a fellow has," I said, "as long as he gets to pick his confirmation name himself." Mary had moved Walter to her shoulder and was patting his back. He let out a hearty belch. She wiped his lips and turned him around for me to see.

"Walter, meet your uncle Cuss. He's the brains of

the family and he reads for fun. Do you want to hold him?" she asked me.

"Nah," I said, taking a step backward.

"Oh, come on, Cuss. Walter's your nephew! Come sit on the bed. You won't drop him." I sat at the end of Mary's bed and she handed the baby to me. "Make sure you don't let his head flop," she said. I took Walter into my arms and held him carefully. "He won't bite you," teased Mary. "Hug him close." I pulled the baby closer. He was heavy and warm and he looked right into my eyes. Despite what Mary had said about hair, he looked as bald as an egg to me. Just like his pa.

"His eyes are blue," I said, surprised. No one in our family had blue eyes.

"Ma says all babies start out with blue eyes," she said. "They turn brown later."

"Oh," I said, staring down at my nephew. I'd never paid attention to babies at all, not human babies, anyway. Calves, puppies, kittens, piglets—I knew all about those. Walter looked sleepy. He waved one fist in the air. "Hey, maybe he'll be a prize-fighter. I'll teach him a few good blocks and punches when he gets bigger."

"Don't you dare," said Mary, and we both laughed.

"He's a nice nephew," I said, handing the baby back to Mary. She kissed his head and cuddled him.

I decided that it was now or never. "Maybe I'll get another nephew out of Matt and Emmeline."

"Matt is counting on a boy the first time around, according to Emmeline," said Mary. "He won't even consider any girls' names." My heart jumped into high gear. *Careful,* I told myself.

"Oh, I bet he'd like a girl as much as a boy," I said. "He'd spoil a girl something awful."

Mary smiled. "Isn't that the truth!" she said, smoothing the front of Walter's little nightgown.

"I sure miss Matt," I said.

"Me, too," said Mary. Her cheeks flushed pink. Was she feeling guilty about why he went away? *Careful,* I told myself again.

"They would have left sooner or later," I said. "Matt talked about it all the time."

"He did?" said Mary. She looked up, surprised. Were those tears in her eyes?

"Oh, yeah," I said, lying through my teeth. "He used to say all the time how one of these days he'd flip a coin. Heads, he'd go north to the Alaska territory; tails, he'd go south to California."

"I didn't know that," she said. "He had the band and everything. I just figured he'd be a miner like everyone else, but then—" She stopped talking and I jumped in to fill the silent gap.

"Nope, not Matt. And Joey, after he'd been to France and all, well, he just couldn't stay put, either." I searched Mary's face. Did she believe me? In for a penny, in for a pound. I took a deep breath. "So, really, getting to California was part of the plan all along." I lowered my voice to make it sound like I was in on the secret.

Mary nodded thoughtfully. She petted Walter's cheek with one finger. Slowly, slowly he closed his eyes and fell asleep.

"I'm glad they got away," said Mary. "California sounds so swell." Her voice was almost a whisper, as though the people out on the road might hear us talking about our brothers. "Emmeline says he loves working in the orchards," said Mary. "She writes to me through her cousin, you know, Bertha Pike? Ma was fit to be tied when I told her. She made me promise not to tell them any bad news, nothing at all. She is so doggone proud. And she wouldn't want them to think they should come home. You know." I nodded. *Keep talking, Mary,* I thought. She took a breath. "Anyhow, maybe they call it groves. Beats me. Matt promised to build Emmeline a house of her own by the end of the year—one with a front porch and an electric cookstove. He could never have bought her an electric stove on a miner's pay, not unless he was a supervisor, like Clement."

Orchards. Hokey-dokey. So they weren't cutting trees after all. Now I knew what kind of work my brothers were doing. Some kind of farming. I fought the urge to wipe the sweat from my palms. I forced my voice to be calm.

"Matt used to call California 'the promised land.' I knew there were a lot of grapes in Napa," I said, "and fruit orchards."

"Nuts, too," said Mary. "Isn't the name of that walnut farm dopey?" I swallowed hard. "I can hardly say it with a straight face."

"Me either," I said, chuckling about a joke I didn't know. *O God, if you're up there, let her say it.* I felt myself praying as hard as I'd ever prayed. Would God listen to a fellow who'd just lied his ears off?

"Farthington's House of Nuts," whispered Mary. "It sounds like a regular loony bin! That's how I address all my letters to Emmeline. I don't write her name on the outside of the envelopes at all. On the inside, on the folded-up letter I write 'Please deliver to Mrs. Matthew Petrovich,' and when Mr. Farthington's secretary opens the envelopes, she makes sure the letters get to Emmeline. Once Mr. Jamison down at the post office asked about the House of Nuts. I nearly had kittens, Cuss. I told him we had a poor, crazy uncle there! You should have seen his face. How's that for quick thinking?" Mary giggled, but I laughed out loud from sheer relief and it woke up Walter.

"Shh! Cuss, jeez! Don't be such an elephant."

"Sorry, sorry." I stood up and waved goodbye. "I was just imagining Mr. Jamison. I'll mosey along now. See you later," I whispered. "Walter is dandy." Mary grinned and I let myself out of the room.

"What did you think?" said Estelle when I got downstairs.

"He's a baby, all right," I said, trying not to jump up and down and shout and grin my fool face in half. "See you around, Estelle," I said. I hopped down the front steps.

"Don't you want your bucket back?" yelled Estelle, but I was already halfway down the block.

"I'll get it later!" I yelled back.

Napa it was. Farthington's House of Nuts. A walnut farm. And Mary had even told me how to send letters! My feet pounded the ground. I felt like jumping in the air like a calf that had just been let out of the barn. This was it. I knew everything I needed to know to get out of Roslyn and find my brothers. I'd write to Matt and tell him everything, and I'd tell him to keep an eye out for a certain visitor—Yours Truly.

I raced toward the colored end of town to tell Perks the big news. We were on our way.

By the end of the day we had all our plans laid out and I had mailed a letter to Matt. In it I told him everything that had happened, down to the last detail. It wasn't right for Ma not to tell him. Her pride had gotten in the way of common sense, and it was high time my brothers knew the score.

I told Matt about Charliehorse and Leroy. And I told him that he and Joey couldn't come back, no matter what, that there were more fights and more rumors than ever. Then I told him I was coming there to work because there wasn't a dime to be earned in Roslyn anymore. I'd folded up the letter and written on the outside "Please deliver to Matthew or Joseph Petrovich." I'd made an envelope out of another piece of paper, put my letter inside, and glued the whole thing shut with flour paste. On the outside I wrote "Farthington's House of Nuts, Napa, California," and mailed it after lunch. The postmaster didn't say a word when I bought a stamp, but I did notice he gave me a funny look.

"Our batty uncle loves mail," I said. Mr. Jamison winked.

*   *   *

Perks and I decided not to breathe a word to Skinny. "He'll be the first one your ma asks when you turn up missing," said Perks.

"And he's rotten at lying," I said. I didn't like skipping town without telling my pal, but there was nothing to be done. The sun was hot and our cows walked at a snail's pace, swishing their tails every couple of steps. Perks's cow, Jezebel, looked skinnier than ever.

"We're gonna need supplies," said Perks. "We gotta bring water, enough to get us to California. Maybe a whole milk can full, maybe more."

"And food," I said. "We'll have to stock up—whatever we can get our hands on."

We walked for a while without talking. The sun had baked the ground, and with each step the cows' feet made little puffs of dry dust. Perks spoke. "Sometimes I gotta pinch myself to remember that it's a real plan. We're gonna do it. We're gonna get outta Roslyn for good and make something outta ourselves."

"It'll take careful planning," I said. "Real careful." We agreed to meet in the barn around midnight to talk some more. Perks headed up the street, leading Jezebel by the halter.

"Git home, girls," I said to the cows, and I gave Geraldine a tap on the behind with the stick I was carrying. She and the other two cows trotted up the hill to our house. I took my time.

When I passed Giombetti's Butcher Shop, Skinny burst out of the front door. He still had on his butcher's apron and the strings flapped behind him. I wiped the sweat off my face with one arm.

"Where's the fire, Skinny?" I said.

"Bad news, Cuss," said Skinny. "The worst ever." His voice cracked and he sniffed. Before I could even ask what the matter was, he blurted out, "Pop's taking us back to Italy. At first when he said it, I thought he was threatening. I thought he was just threatening!"

"Are you sure?"

"Swear to God," said Skinny. He crossed himself and then the tears started to fall. He swiped at his eyes with his arm. "The mines laid off upward of two hundred men so far, and Pop says we'll starve if this keeps up. And he has this uncle-somebody who has a butcher shop in Milan. I don't want to go to Milan! I'm an American! I don't even speak Italian that good." Skinny sniffled and wiped his nose with the back of his hand.

"Don't be such a girl," I said. "This calls for clear thinking."

"What thinking?" said Skinny. "Pop says we go to Milan, we go to Milan." He took a deep gulp of the hot afternoon air and mopped his brow. A fly landed on the front of his bloody apron.

"I can drill you on cuss words," I said, trying to be funny.

Skinny wiped the tears away with the back of his hand and shook his head. "It's no use," he said. "I'm no good at Italian. I don't want to live where everyone speaks Italian. I don't want to go to school in Italian!"

"I know a way for you to stay in America," I said. The words slid out before I could stop them. I glanced up the hill and saw Philip coming toward us. "Meet me up in our barn," I said. "In the hayloft, at midnight tonight. Me and Perks'll be waiting."

"Are you crazy?" said Skinny.

"No," I said. "Are you? You want to go to Italy? Or do you want to stay in America?" Skinny stared and didn't say anything. I nodded toward Philip. "I can't talk now. Tonight it is."

"Cuss!" hollered Philip. "Hurry up! Ma's been holding supper for half an hour."

I said so long to Skinny and hustled toward home with my fingers and toes crossed. Perks wasn't going to like it, but Skinny was in desperate straits. And three boys was only one more than two.

As soon as Perks climbed up into the hayloft that night, I gave him the lowdown on Skinny. He was peeved when I told him I'd invited Skinny until I explained the situation about his family going back to Italy. "Hell's bells," said Perks, and he let out a low whistle. "That's bad luck. But he better not spill the beans, that's all I'm saying about it."

When we told Skinny the plan, his mouth dropped open. "Are you two out of your skulls?"

"I told you we shouldn't tell him," whispered Perks. It was dark in the hayloft, but enough moonlight came in to make a faint outline of his head and face.

"Stuff it, Perks," I said. "It's not crazy, Skinny. Guys do this all the time when they're flat broke. It's the American way. We gotta find work, and there's nothing here."

Skinny lifted his cap and scratched his head. His curls were growing back. "What if we get caught?" he asked.

"What if we don't?" asked Perks. "We live in California like a bunch of fat cats."

"We'd go to jail," said Skinny.

"The slammer's for criminals," said Perks. "We're just boys having fun."

"Jumping a train is against the law," said Skinny. "It's a sin."

"It ain't a sin," said Perks. "You ever heard of 'Thou Shalt Not Jump the Train'?"

"No," said Skinny.

"Then it ain't a sin," said Perks.

"Enough with the catechism lesson," I said. "Skinny, we're gonna meet behind Marko's the night after they unload all the grapes. The train leaves the next morning, first thing. If you're with us, bring as much food as you can carry, and water. That's the long and short of it."

Skinny was quiet.

"Well?" I said.

"I don't want to go to Milan," he said.

"There's no beefsteaks on this trip," said Perks. "Don't forget. Just a whole lotta apples and some old bread, and buckets of warm water."

"You saying I ain't tough enough?" said Skinny.

"Ain't saying nothing of the sort," said Perks. "Next time we meet on the sly like this, it will be on account of a certain train is in town."

"First night in town it's full of grapes," I said. "So we steer clear. Too many eyes."

"Yeah," said Skinny. "A lot of guys out trying to snatch a box or two. Next day they sell grapes until they're gone, which is usually afternoon, maybe sooner. Then they clean out and leave first thing the next morning."

"Then it's all aboard the second night," said Perks. "We gotta all be ready."

"I'm as ready as I'll ever be," I said, but I sounded more ready than I felt. Soon we'd be in California. I'd see Matt and Joey again. The thought made me grin, and it crowded out the other thoughts of leaving Ma and the rest of my family behind, maybe forever. I was doing this for them. I couldn't wait around on the off chance that the mines would hire me someday soon. I had to take my chances. Matt would understand that. As soon as I found my brothers, everything would be square again.

"I'm in," said Skinny. "Anything is better than Italy. And I'll bring pepperonis."

He dug in his pocket and pulled out something small. He held his hand under a streak of moonlight so we could see it was an Indian-head nickel.

"I swear not to tell a soul," Skinny said, spitting on the nickel. He rubbed his thumb on the spit. "And I swear to stay pals with you two knuckleheads for the rest of my life."

"I swear, too," said Perks in a whisper. He spit and rubbed the nickel.

"I swear, too," I said.

We finished by deciding what food to bring and how to carry it, and how we'd stash it the night before behind Marko's. We shook hands all around and climbed down the ladder in silence. Perks and Skinny waved and headed toward the road without a sound.

Chapter Thirty

The days dragged on, hot and dusty and long. There was no telling exactly what day the grape train would chug into town, so I worked in the garden and in the barn and tried to keep busy so I wouldn't think about it all the time. There was no other choice but to leave, no other way to get money to my family. Every day the mines laid off more men.

Father Duval came by on a Thursday evening. Philip and I were up on the barn roof, fixing a hole in the tin.

"Hello up there," called Father Duval from the front porch.

"Hello, Father," I called down.

"I wonder what he wants," said Philip, cutting a piece of tin with the tin snips.

"Probably someone to help with funeral duty," I said, mostly to myself.

"Ma's gonna have a fit," said Philip. "You know how she is when the priest shows up. She gets all fluttery." I nodded and grinned.

A while later Father Duval emerged from the house. "*Dobra večer!*" he yelled. *Good evening.*

"*Dobra večer* to you, too!" I hollered. Philip must have read my lips.

"Father Duval talks Czech at Pinky's house," he said.

"Father Duval likes languages," I said, making sure Philip understood me.

He scowled. "I don't know why," said Philip. That I didn't try to explain.

My guess about Father Duval's visit was right. There was a funeral scheduled for the next day, and Ma had signed me up.

"Mrs. Felini," said Ma in Croatian. "She was ninety-two. Always missed Italy, though I can't imagine why. May she rest in peace." Ma crossed herself and then she looked at me. I realized for the first time how much taller than her I had grown. "Do you like to help at the funerals?"

"I s'pose," I said. "I like weddings better, though." There was even more food at a wedding, and dancing to boot. Ma nodded and looked like she was about to say something else, but then she turned away quickly and stirred a pot on the stove.

This would probably be my last funeral. Ma didn't know that. Neither did Father Duval. There were plenty of boys who could help out at church. I was on to bigger things. I hoped Mrs. Felini's relatives were good cooks.

The funeral was a dandy, with lots of food, especially cold cuts.

"Without your help, Slava," said Father Duval as he loaded me up with leftovers, "I would have to change my name to Father Hippo." He laughed and patted his belly. The buttons were tight across the front of his black cassock. I laughed with him, but only out of politeness. He'd find someone else when I was gone.

On the way home I sorted out the food that I thought would keep for a train trip: two loops of dried pepperoni and a round cheese still in its skin. I put everything in a gunnysack when I got home and tucked the bundle into a hole in the back wall of the cellar. It felt a little like stealing, but hadn't Father Duval given it to me to give to the family? I was part of the family, so if I kept some for myself, it could hardly be a sin. That was what I told myself, but I still felt like the cat who ate the canary. I didn't know how much food we'd need because I didn't know how long the train ride would take. Maybe that was something Perks could find out.

The next day was Saturday. Philip and I picked and pitted all the plums from one of Ma's trees and then laid them out to dry on gunnysacks that we spread out in a sunny spot. If they were dry by the time the grape train came, I'd take some along.

After supper, Mary stopped by with little Walter and the latest copy of the *Miner's Echo*. She and Ma sat on the front porch and visited in Croatian. I read the paper and listened with one ear.

"Everyone's leaving town," said Mary. "Clement says they're hiring longshoremen in Tacoma." She shifted Walter to one shoulder and patted his back.

"Katja's two boys are going," said Ma. They talked about cousins and second cousins who were leaving. Mary knew someone who was going back to the Old Country.

"If the mines don't keep up production, I don't know what we'll do," said Mary. "Clement's job is safe, at least for now."

Ma reached out and Mary handed the baby to her. Ma rocked little Walter until he went to sleep. She and Mary chatted quietly about babies and how to cure bellyache and what to do for diaper rash. I read until it was too dark to see.

Just before bed I found Ma busy in the kitchen. I gave her a hug, and when I pulled away, I noticed that her face was wet with tears. "All the big boys are leaving town," she said in Croatian. "They are so impatient! But you wait, Slava. The mines will hire again and you will be ready. You will be first in line for a full-time job!" She patted me on the shoulder and whispered, "Are you still wishing to stay in school?" She searched my face with her red, tired eyes.

"No," I said. "School is for rich people."

Ma nodded. "Good. That is what I told him," she said.

"Told who?" I asked.

"The holy priest," she said.

"Father Duval?" I said. "I haven't said anything to him about quitting school."

"I talked to him about it," said Ma. That was news to me. I must have had surprise written all over my mug, because Ma explained before I had a chance to ask.

"When he came the other evening," Ma said, "I confessed to him that I was ashamed of the charity, the food he was sending home. I told him there are poorer widows than me in this town. Father Duval said that he wanted to make sure you stayed in school, that I didn't put you to work like the other boys your age."

By this time my mouth was hanging open. Father Duval wanted me to stay in school, and that was the reason for all the funeral and wedding jobs? Ma kept on talking, almost to herself more than to me.

"I said you were finished with school, that you have the most school of anyone in our family, that more schooling is for families with money, not for us. He said he understood, and he promised to say prayers for our family. He said if you work for him, if you work for the church at a funeral or wedding, you deserve something, so the food is not charity, it is your wages, and that as long as you can help him, he will pay you in food, until you get a job that pays wages. That is only fair. So I agreed—you work for Father whenever he wants. At least it is something."

"Funeral food isn't enough, Ma," I said. "It won't pay your mortgage."

Ma closed her eyes and bit her lower lip as though she were in pain.

"Ma?"

"I am going to lose the house, Slava. It is certain."

"But—" I said, but Ma cut me off with a shake of her head.

"You might as well know it. Don't tell Philip. He is sad enough as it is. I don't have the money to pay the bank. Even if I sold the cows . . . everything. No, it is God's will." Ma's eyes filled with new tears. She wiped them away with the back of her hand and tried to smile. It was a rotten attempt.

I lay awake in bed that night and thought about how the attic used to be full of us boys. I was tired of God's will always ending up as our bad luck. I was about to make some good luck of my own. Ma wouldn't like it, and maybe God wouldn't, either. One thing was sure. Once I got on that train, there would be no turning back.

Chapter Thirty-One

Father Duval sent word early the next morning that he needed an altar boy for Sunday mass, so at six-thirty I was on my way to the church. Turned out my cousin Putzy was on the list but didn't show up on account of he'd gotten into a wasp's nest and wasn't in any condition to go anywhere. I did my duties as usual, but my mind was a thousand miles away in California, so Father's announcement of a second collection for a mission school near Walla Walla caught me off-guard. I was on my feet and ready to carry out the cross when I realized he was still talking. The ushers came forward with the collection baskets. I felt my face turn red and sat back down.

Afterward, while we took off our albs, I wondered if Father Duval would scold me for daydreaming, but he didn't say a word about it. A little girl about six years old came into the sacristy without knocking. She was pale and out of breath. She bobbed a curtsy and tugged on Father's cassock.

"Grandmama says to bring you." Her dark eyes filled with tears. "The baby's sick and he ain't baptized yet."

Father Duval placed his hand on the little girl's head. "Straightaway," he said, and he left his stole in place. He put his chasuble on the chair. "You show me to your house, yes?" She nodded and headed out the door into the church. Father Duval grabbed his hat off its hook and said, "You boys put everything away. Slava, I leave you in charge."

"Yes, Father," I said, glad I'd escaped a chewing-out. I hung my alb on the nail in the altar boys' closet and then picked up Father's chasuble and hung it in his closet.

"Should I do something?" asked the other altar boy. He was Philip's age, a kid named Arnold Zmecki, just a little shrimp starting out.

"Nah, I'll do the rest," I said. Arnold slipped out the back door.

If the grape train came soon, I'd probably never be back here again, I thought as I straightened Arnold's alb on the other nail. That was when I spied the two collection baskets. They were stacked in one corner of the counter where Father kept his books, one on top of the other. Usually Father Duval took them with him into the rectory right after Sunday mass. He'd been in such a hurry, though, that he'd left without finishing up.

The top basket had a piece of paper on top. It had the words "Mission Collection" written in pencil. I wondered how much money folks would cough up on a Sunday morning in August.

I lifted the two baskets. They were heavy with coins. I knew Ma put in a nickel every week even when we couldn't afford it. Had she given two nickels this week, one for the mission? We didn't have an extra penny, let alone an extra ten cents. But who was I to tell Ma what to do with the little money she did have? If things went according to our plans, she'd soon have more. Maybe someday she'd even have enough to put four bits in the collection.

It wouldn't do to leave money out on the counter. I put the two baskets on the floor of the vestments closet and shut the door. Father Duval would be sure to find them later when he put away his stole.

I looked around for the last time. I'd seen a lot of this place lately. Lord knew there were plenty of boys in Roslyn who would fill my shoes when I was gone. I felt bad that Ma wouldn't get any more funeral food, but once I'd earned enough to pay off Ma's mortgage, it wouldn't matter one bit.

I closed the door and walked out into the church. Some old ladies were praying the rosary in Italian. I genuflected, dipped my finger in the holy-water font, crossed myself, hurried out the door, and ran down the stairs of the church. I'd been baptized there. I'd had my First Communion and had been confirmed there. I'd never missed Sunday mass, except for the week I had measles. I'd seen plenty of funerals and weddings, and Ma had dragged me to every Holy Day mass on the Church calendar, except for when Philip was sick. Except for home and school, there wasn't a single building in Roslyn that I'd spent more time in. I'd never thought about it before like that. If the grape train came that week, I'd never step foot in that church again. I didn't look back.

It was hot all day and it didn't cool off when the sun dipped behind the mountains. Philip and I milked the cows and swatted at the flies. Geraldine smacked me in the head with her tail. I swore and wiped the sweat from my face. And then a train whistle blew, long and loud.

It wasn't the sound of the passenger train, and it wasn't the sound of a coal train. It was just like I'd remembered it from the year before. The grape train was back.

I carried two buckets of milk onto the porch and set them down. I told myself to be calm, or at least to look calm. If anyone'd said boo to me just then, I would have jumped out of my skin. I blew out a lungful of air and hocked a loogie into the dirt. The whistle blew again when I was on my way into the house.

"The train is late today," said Ma. She and Mary were in the kitchen peeling potatoes. Little Walter slept in a basket on the floor.

"It's not the passenger train," I said.

"No," said Mary. "Clement left on the passenger train. He's going to Spokane. Something to do with the mining company. Walter and I are going to stay here for a few days."

"It's the grape train," I said. "Probably." I knew it was the grape train. The grape-train whistle didn't sound like any other train whistle. A year before, that same grape train had changed everything. I wondered if Mary remembered the sound, too. Now the grape train was about to change things again.

I ate in a hurry, forcing myself to fill up on applesauce and bread and plums and potatoes, even though I wasn't hungry. Ma had gone off to Pinky's house without eating. His ma was sick. Mary served dinner and chatted while we ate, but I hardly heard her. Walter woke up and she stopped to feed him, and then we didn't talk at all, and it was a good thing. I had an urge to spill the beans and ruin everything.

When me and Perks and Skinny had had our planning meeting in the hayloft, we'd figured that on account of the trip being a long one, we'd need all the water we could get, and that meant more containers than we could fill and carry in one night. It'd been Perks's idea to get ready the night before, to store everything behind the grocery store and fill the buckets at Marko's pump the second night right before we got into the boxcar. I thought over our plan while I strained the milk and washed the buckets. I hoped Big Swede would be drunk and busy with other boys trying to steal grapes.

Before she'd left, Ma had asked me to churn a gallon of cream into butter. After that, Philip and I shooed some of our chickens down out of a tree and into the hen house, and then we closed all the chickens in for the night. I worked with only half my brain. The other half was on our plan.

Ma came home looking pretty down in the mouth. I didn't want to think about how she'd look when I was gone, too. Ma put her hand on Philip's shoulder and made sure he could see her face. "Pinky's mama died," she said in English. Philip understood. He hung his head and Ma gave him a hug. "TB," Ma said to me.

Pinky's mom had always been sickly. Ma had taken her beet soup more than once. I felt sorry for Pinky, but I was too excited and worried and eager about the grape train to care as much as I should have. Philip sniffled and wiped his nose on his shoulder. I poured myself some cold coffee and wondered if I'd stocked enough food for the long trip to California.

Later, while we were lying in bed, Philip elbowed me and said, "Will you be an altar boy at Pinky's ma's funeral? I know Pinky will ask for you if you want."

"I s'pose," I said, nodding. There was enough moonlight in the room for Philip to see my face. How could I tell the squirt that in less than forty-eight hours I'd be long gone?

"Ma will probably help, huh, Cuss?" I nodded so Philip would know I was listening. Ma often helped fix up dead folks for their wake and funeral, just like she helped when babies were born. I thought about the pepperonis Skinny had promised to bring. Pepperoni made a fellow thirsty. Would we need extra water if we ate pepperoni?

"I bet Father Duval said prayers at Pinky's, like when I was sick. Only Pinky's mom didn't make it." Philip sniffled and it turned into coughing.

"Pinky'll be all right," I said. "He has a bunch of sisters." Philip frowned and tried hard to understand me. "Sisters," I repeated. "They'll fuss over him."

"Sisters ain't the same as a mother," said Philip. "And sisters ain't the same as a brother, either."

Even in the dim light I could see that Philip's eyes were shiny with tears. I grinned and poked him in the nose. He grinned back, slugged me in the arm, then turned on his side and was quiet after that. I listened until I could tell by his breathing that he was asleep. How would Philip get along without me? I hadn't thought about that before. The kid was going to miss me. And I'd miss him. But I had no choice.

The clock chimed out eleven-fifteen, eleven-thirty. Eleven-forty-five. I crawled out of bed and pulled on my overalls. I tiptoed over to the closet and lifted up the winter blanket in the corner where I'd hidden an old gunnysack and filled it with my things. I brought it out without making a sound.

Inside the gunnysack I had eighty cents wrapped tight in a sock so it wouldn't make noise. I had my poetry book wrapped in a shirt, one pair of knickers, and Matt's old boots with the toes cut so my feet would fit. I'd cleaned and shined Pa's fancy shoes and put them under our bed. Maybe Philip could wear them someday.

My jackknife was already in my pocket. I'd

stowed another gunnysack in the barn, full of apples and dried plums and all the other food I'd been keeping in the cellar. I'd patched an old, leaky milk can to use for water. It was in the barn, too. All I had to do that night was get my gear downtown and stowed. The next night we'd fill the buckets with water, load our supplies, and wave goodbye to Roslyn.

I crept down the stairs. I listened for Ma but didn't hear a peep. I fought the urge to clear my throat. The last thing I needed was to wake up little Walter and set him to screaming. The screen door squeaked. I froze and half expected Ma to call out. I let myself out of the house, got the food bundle and milk can from the barn, and headed down to Marko's Grocery.

Chapter Thirty-Two

Even in the dark the letters on the sides of the boxcars were easy to read: BLACK BEAR WINE GRAPES—NAPA, CALIFORNIA. I took a deep breath and was sure I could smell the grapes in the hot night air. There were four boxcars and an engine. Down at the end of the line I saw the red caboose. Would we really make it all the way to California without being nabbed? Matt and Joey had done it. We could do it, too. I hurried through the shadows to the stacks of boxes and barrels behind Marko's.

"What took you so long?" said Perks. "I already got my supplies into one of the barrels, safe and sound for tomorrow night." He grinned and slugged me in the shoulder. "See our ride to freedom out there?"

"Yeah, I saw it," I said. Just then Skinny showed up. He had three large pepperonis in his arms.

"I had to swipe these," he whispered. "I don't think Pop'll miss them." Skinny sounded worried. I figured his conscience was bothering him. I felt a warning prickle at the back of my neck. If Skinny got to blabbing out of guilt, we'd be stuck in Roslyn forever.

"Swipe sausage or go back to wopland," said Perks. "Sounds like an easy choice to me." He piled the pepperonis into the barrel along with my gunny-sack. "Where's the rest of your gear?" Perks asked Skinny.

"I'll bring it tomorrow," said Skinny.

We sat on the ground in the shadows and spoke in whispers.

"Big Swede is the bull on duty," said Perks. "Two bits says he'll be around tomorrow night, too, when the boxcars are empty. So we'll have to run like the devil when we get on the train." Skinny wiped sweat from his forehead. He was as nervous as a cat on ice. "With all the grapes gone," said Perks, "Big Swede won't be so watchful."

"He's on the lookout tonight, though," said Skinny, licking his lips. "Too bad we can't try for some grapes. I can smell 'em."

"You can get all the grapes you want in California," I said.

"Shut up, you knuckleheads," said Perks. "There he is!" We watched as Big Swede came slowly down the side of the train, nightstick in hand.

"He don't look drunk this time," said Skinny.

Big Swede passed in front of the train and walked around behind on the side we couldn't see. I crossed my fingers and hoped Big Swede would find his way into Slim's bar the next night.

I was jammed between Perks and Skinny, and I could smell their sweat and feel the heat from their bodies. We watched Big Swede make three rounds. No one said a word. I wondered if Perks and Skinny were thinking what I was thinking. Once we got on that train, there was no turning back.

The town clock struck one and Perks jumped. "I gotta get back to the cafe," he said. "Can't believe I sat here daydreaming about oranges and palm trees and piles of greenbacks so high." He brushed off the seat of his overalls. "I gotta close the cafe," he said. "Tomorrow night'll be the last time."

Skinny and I got to our feet. "See you boys tomorrow night, then," I said. "Two-thirty A.M. Train leaves before dawn. That'll give us time to get loaded up and settled in."

"I can't hardly wait to get going," said Perks.

"Me, neither," I whispered.

"Me, neither," said Skinny, but I wasn't convinced. Perks saluted and ran off, dodging the lit places and keeping to the shadows.

"See you later," I said to Skinny. He nodded. That worried prickle got my attention again. "Don't let the cat out of the bag, Skinny."

"I'm no snitch," said Skinny.

"I know," I said. "Just making sure." I slid Skinny's cap off his head and smacked him with it. He grabbed his hat out of my hands and jammed it back on his head. I let him punch me in the arm, whispered, "So long," and then I hurried through town.

Our house was quiet and dark. Even so, as I walked toward it, I kept to the shadowy places where the big trees kept the moonlight from reaching the ground. I saw Lucky the cat slink out from under the barn door and disappear into the night. I wondered what he was after. All the sneaking around and excitement about our getaway gave me a big reason to stop at the outhouse before making my way back into the house. The outhouse door creaked open on its hinges.

"Hey!" yelled my sister, Mary. All I saw was the white of her nightgown. I jumped back and let the

outhouse door slam shut. My heart hammered in my chest. The outhouse door opened up.

"Give a girl a little warning, would ya?" said Mary.

"Sorry," I said. "I thought it was empty." My hands trembled from the surprise. I shoved them in my pockets.

Mary stepped out. "Have you been out stealing grapes?" she whispered. "Clement says all the boys try. The train's in town tonight, isn't it?"

"Yeah," I said, forcing my voice to sound as normal as pie. "But I wasn't stealing grapes. Now, I gotta do some business, Mary," I said, shutting the outhouse door. When I finished, she was waiting for me, leaning against the trunk of a skinny pine tree a few feet from the outhouse.

"It was a year ago that Matt and Joey had to leave," whispered Mary. "Remember?"

I walked toward the house and Mary fell in beside me. "I remember," I said.

"They got clean away," said Mary. "You don't know how hard I prayed that they would. It was awful, Cuss." My sister stopped and stared up at the sky. I stopped, too. This I wanted to hear—anything at all about how Matt and Joey got away. In a few hours it would be me getting away. "Did you ever try to count the stars?" asked Mary.

"Once," I said. I didn't want to jaw about stars. I swallowed and took a chance. "Perks said he heard that Joey and Matt hopped the grape train last year."

"Well, they didn't exactly hop it," said Mary. "But they didn't ride first class, either, if you know what I mean." I stood stock-still and held my breath. "They paid, you know, under the table. Twenty-six dollars apiece."

"They paid to ride the grape train?" I saw Mary nod.

"Clement arranged the whole thing, on account of he knows a lot of the railroad boys. Matt and Joey paid Big Swede and he split the money with the brakeman, who let them ride in the caboose all the way to California. So they didn't really *hop* the train." My mouth had gone as dry as old leaves. Mary started up the stairs to the back door, but I grabbed her hand.

"Why didn't they just hop it?" I asked. "Hopping would've been free." I tried to whisper, but my voice came out in squeaks.

"It isn't a direct train, that's why, silly. They would've been caught for sure. It goes out to Seattle and loads up with other freight. Then the whole train heads south. I was so relieved when we got that first letter." I stood frozen in place as Mary tiptoed up the rest of the stairs and let herself into the house. She turned around. "Come on in the house, Cuss. And don't wake Walter."

It hurt to swallow. My pulse pounded in my ears. *Twenty-six bucks apiece.*

I spun around and ran as hard as I could. I heard Mary say, "Hey! Cuss!" But I didn't stop. I ran down the hill toward town and didn't even slow down when I got to the main street. I didn't care who saw me. The only people out at that time of night were soused anyhow. I ran north to the colored part of town, stopping only when I got to the back door of the cafe. I knocked and prayed that Perks would answer.

"Cuss," said my pal, opening the door. "You look like you seen a ghost." He pulled me into the back room. The light from the electric bulb made me squint. My breath came in big gasps. My chest heaved in and out, and when I tried to talk, the words came out cracked.

"Matt and Joey," I said, fighting to get enough air to talk. "They paid Big Swede. They paid to ride the grape train to California."

Perks's mouth dropped open. "It's a lie."

"Mary told me," I said. I took a big gulp of air. "Twenty-six bucks apiece. It ain't a direct train, Perks. It goes to Seattle and reloads." We stared at each other. Perks let out a long, low whistle and shook his head slowly from side to side.

"That complicates the plan," he said finally.

"Complicates?" I said, and my voice squeaked. "Did you hear me? Twenty-six bucks! Might as well be a thousand. We ain't going *anywhere*."

Perks's sister Mildred came into the kitchen with a load of dirty dishes.

"No playing around, Percy," she scolded. She looked dead tired as she put the plates and silverware beside the dishpan. She saw me, but she didn't bother to say hello. "Ma wants out of here by two, hear?"

"I heard," said Perks, but I could tell his mind wasn't on dishes. As soon as Mildred was out of earshot, he said, "We're leaving on that grape train."

"You're full of beans, Perks," I said. "We'd have to rob a bank to get the money."

"I got my connections," he said. "What about your rich uncle—the one who sells bohunk brew? Maybe he'd loan you the dough. How much money you got of your own?"

"Eighty cents," I said. "That's it."

Perks grabbed me by both shoulders and pulled me close. We were eye to eye and I could smell his breath and his sweat. "Cuss," he said, "we got one chance to get outta this town and find real jobs."

"But it's twenty-six bucks apiece," I said, squirming free.

"You think I like seeing my mama and all my sisters working until two, three, every morning just to put money in somebody else's pockets? And all my sisters, big and little, working in this hole?"

I thought about Ma scrubbing dirty laundry, scrimping and scraping just to feed us. And now she was going to lose the house. Philip might never work for wages. It was all up to me.

"I'm gonna find me that money if I have to beg, borrow, or steal," said Perks. "I'm getting out, and my mama is gonna own this cafe someday." His eyes were bright and the grin had crept onto his face again. "There ain't no other way, Cuss. You with me? Are we going to California?"

"Maybe Uncle Tony would loan me something," I said. "Or Mary."

"Skinny could loan us the money. For certain he's got enough for himself and us, too," said Perks.

I shook my head. "I don't know if he has any money of his own," I said, "besides the nickel he carries around."

"I got fourteen dollars and six bits hid safe and sound in a jar in the ground behind the outhouse," said Perks. "I was gonna dig it up anyhow. All's I need is eleven bucks, two bits, and I'm all set. I'll get it."

"Even if we had the money, we'd have to do a deal with Big Swede," I said.

"That's nothing," said Perks, and his voice had that old familiar bragging sound to it. "Dealing with Big Swede is just nothing. You leave that to me and my connections. What we gotta do is come up with a few dollars and cents."

"You make it sound so smooth," I said, feeling hot under the collar. "Just scare up some fast cash, that's all. That's why we're skipping town in the first place—because there ain't no money."

"We got twenty-four hours, more or less," said Perks. "And this skinny boy is getting on that grape train, whether his best pal goes with him or not. If you're too chicken to try, too proud to ask for a loan, that's your problem, not mine. You can stay in Roslyn if you want, but count me out. Now, I gotta do some dishes before Mildred takes the broom to my behind." He turned away and stuck his hands into the dishpan.

"I'll think about it," I said.

Perks didn't look up. "You already think too much, Cuss. It's *doing* that counts in a pinch. And pal, this here is a pinch."

I left the cafe and headed home. Halfway up the hill all the tiredness caught up with me. Twenty-six bucks. It was hopeless. I'd never even had five bucks of my own. I couldn't ask Uncle Tony or Mary. They'd rat on me and Ma would dish out a licking I'd never forget. I kicked a stone. The town clock struck two.

I looked up the hill and saw our little house against the moonlit sky. It wasn't much, just a box with windows and a roof and a front porch, but it was Ma's, the only property she'd ever owned. It was the reason she and Pa had come to America, the reason she'd left her own parents in the Old Country forever.

I heard the whoosh of an owl's wings as it flew over my head, and I looked up to see it fly to the top of a tall pine tree next to the church. In the few seconds that it took to watch the owl, I knew I would be on the grape train when it pulled out of Roslyn, and I knew how I would get the money to do it.

Chapter Thirty-Three

Immaculate Conception Church was never locked. I pulled open the door just wide enough to slide in. The tabernacle candle shone red through the lamp glass. I let my eyes adjust. The hair on my arms stood straight up. I got a prickly feeling at the back of my neck, and my palms were so cold and clammy that I thought they might drip.

I genuflected, half out of habit, half out of terror. What I was about to do probably counted as a quadruple mortal sin. I stood in front of the altar and said a quick prayer. "It's only a loan," I whispered. "I'll pay it back, with interest. I'm borrowing." I was breathing hard. I could go to hell for this. I gritted my teeth and swallowed. A trickle of sweat crawled down the side of my face. I tiptoed back toward the sacristy as quiet as any cat burglar.

The two collection baskets were still in the closet. Just like I'd figured, Father Duval had had a busy day, what with the baby and then Pinky's ma. I picked up the baskets and carried them over to a spot where moonlight shone through a little window. I sat on the floor, separated the two baskets, and began to count. My hands shook like I had the fever chills.

There was forty-three dollars and eighty-nine cents between the two collections—a king's ransom. I counted out twenty-six, most of it in coins, and divided the rest between the two baskets. I put ten dollar bills and some change in one, and the rest in the other. Then I stuffed the money into my two front pockets and put the baskets back in the vestments closet, one on top of the other.

I wiped my hands on my overalls. My pockets bulged. I took a deep breath. I waited and listened for a second, just to make sure no one was around, half wondering if lightning would strike me dead. When nothing happened, I let myself out the back door.

The money was heavy in my pockets. No matter how carefully I walked, it jingled with every step until I jammed my hands down in there and held it all still. The coins were hard and my hands were wet.

I'd pay it back, every dime. I'd pay back double, maybe even triple.

I found a rag in the barn and wrapped up the money in it. Then I stuffed it behind a board in the hayloft. I pushed some loose hay over in front of the board. No one would know it was there. No one but me.

The clock struck a quarter after two. In fifteen minutes I'd gone from being a pretty good fellow who swore sometimes but mostly stayed out of trouble to a criminal of the worst kind, even worse than a mobster. Mobsters mostly stole from each other. I'd filched the Sunday collection.

I told myself a hundred times that it was just a loan, but I knew the sheriff wouldn't believe me. Worse than that, I knew if they ever found out, Ma and Father Duval wouldn't believe me, either. I'd make sure no one would ever know. That was the other thing I told myself.

I was on my own from here on out.

Chapter Thirty-Four

I didn't sleep a wink. When it was time to get up, I grabbed a cup of coffee, gulped it down, and went outside to do my chores. Ma didn't ask any questions, and Mary didn't mention our conversation from the middle of the night. It was a good thing. I couldn't have looked either of them in the eye.

I took the three cows up to the hills. Looking back at the town, I could see the grape train. It wasn't even seven o'clock and there were already folks lined up for their grapes. Mr. Marko was going to do a fine bit of business today.

After turning the cows loose for the day, I moseyed back into town. Ma wouldn't expect me. She'd think I was looking for work. I wandered to the back of Marko's Grocery and mixed in with the crowd. Twice I glanced to where our getaway goods were stashed. We'd stacked a broken crate on top of the barrel and leaned half of an oak pallet against it in front. It looked like a pile of junk and matched the other empty barrels and crates and boxes laying around on the ground. No one would know. No one would suspect. I headed to the butcher shop.

Skinny was at the counter with a customer. There was no one else in sight. "There's a complication," I said in a low voice. I nodded in the direction of Marko's Grocery. "We have to pay Big Swede—twenty-six bucks each. Can you get it?"

"What?" asked Skinny. He looked from side to side and licked his lips. He wiped his hands on his apron and came around the counter.

"We can't hop it," I said. "It reloads in Seattle. Twenty-six bucks to go to California in the caboose. You got that much?"

Skinny swallowed and nodded and swatted at a fly on his arm. "I can get it," said Skinny.

"So bring it with you. Perks'll take care of the doing."

Just then Helen pushed through the swinging doors with a tray of chops. "Pop says to mark these down to eighteen cents a pound," she said.

"Hokey-dokey," said Skinny. He watched Helen

leave. When the coast was clear, he turned to me. "Twenty-six bucks?" he said. "Hell's bells."

"I know it's a lot of dough," I said. "But we can't take a chance on getting caught."

"Yeah, you're right," he said, but he didn't look at me. Just then Mr. Giombetti started yelling in Italian from the back room. "I gotta go," said Skinny.

"Tonight, then," I said.

"Yeah, yeah. Right," Skinny said, then turned. "Oh, Cuss," he said, "Father Duval was looking for you." He disappeared through the doors before I could say a word.

For a second I stood there like my feet were nailed to the floor. Father Duval couldn't know about the money. How could he? He hadn't counted it; he'd run out the door with the little girl before he'd had a chance to count it. I thought back to the morning. No, he hadn't touched the collection baskets. Could he have seen me?

It was hot in the butcher shop. If Father Duval had seen me take the money, he'd have said something. He would have caught me then and there, or he would have come to our house, told Ma, asked for it back. No, Father Duval didn't know a thing. I pushed through the door and walked out onto the street. He probably needed someone to help with Pinky's ma's funeral. That had to be it.

The thought pestered me all the way home. Mix that with the bad feeling I had about Skinny, and it was easy to understand why I was in a state. I shrugged it all off as nothing but a bad case of the jitters. Skinny'd be there when it was time to say so long to Roslyn. He didn't want to go to Italy, and he'd spit on the nickel. Father Duval probably just needed someone for a funeral. No sweat.

Lunch that day was cold potatoes and the last bit of funeral salami. Philip said Pinky's cousins would be altar boys at the funeral, so they didn't need me after all.

I tried to eat, tried to fill up, but the food felt like stones in my belly. Mary ate with Walter on her lap. Ma looked older than I'd ever seen her. A fly buzzed above our heads. A piece of potato caught in my throat and I started to choke. Philip thumped me on the back, and Ma handed me my cup of coffee. They didn't know I wouldn't be around tomorrow. They didn't know I had food hidden behind Marko's. They didn't know I'd swiped money from the collection baskets and that Father Duval was looking for me. I felt like a heel, like a crook on the run, fooling everyone, acting like nothing was up.

The rest of the day dragged on. Hour after hour the town clock chimed. I had to use the outhouse more than usual. The day was so hot I felt feverish. It took me twice as long to find the cows. Coming down the hill toward town, I saw that the crowd around the grape train was gone. The cars were standing open and empty. By dawn the grape train would be on its way, and so would I.

That night, after I thought Philip was asleep, I got a piece of paper and a stub of pencil out of my box of school things in the closet. I found a spot on the floor where the moon was shining in and began to write in Croatian.

> Dear Ma,
> When you get this I'll be on my way to earning a decent wage. There's no work in this town for me, and things aren't going to change. The only way to make money is to get out, to find a job someplace else. A lot of guys are leaving, and I'm one of them. I'm going to find Matt and Joey, so don't worry. I know where they are now. As soon as I get paid, I'll send you all the money and maybe you won't lose the house.

Just then Philip spoke. "What are you doing, Cuss?"

I just about jumped out of my skin. "Writing, you dope," I said, leaning my head over into the light and pointing at the paper. "It's Latin. *Latin.* Get it?"

Philip nodded. "How come you're writing Latin? School's over," said Philip. His voice was sleepy and soft. He yawned.

"I don't want to forget it, that's all," I said under my breath. Philip frowned slightly, then closed his eyes. In seconds he was asleep again. My heart was going a mile a minute. I took a deep breath and finished the letter.

There isn't any other way. Try not to be too upset. I'll send you a letter soon.

Volim te,

Slava

One lousy tear dripped off the end of my nose and spotted the page. I wiped it away with my thumb and folded up the letter and placed it under my pillow on the bed. I lay down beside Philip and stared at the ceiling. The wind was blowing outside. I heard it rustle the leaves of the fruit trees and whistle past the roof. A cat meowed. Pinky's dog, Stinker, yapped a few times and then was quiet. The clock struck one.

I watched the patch of moonlight on the floor and I would swear I saw it shifting as the moon rose in the sky. The clock struck one-thirty. And then one-forty-five. Philip turned toward me and I froze, until I saw that he was sound asleep. Even with just the moon-light in our room, I could see the freckles on his nose.

I got up and pulled on my overalls. "'Bye, squirt," I whispered, then I tiptoed down the stairs and out the back door.

The money was right where I'd left it. I stuffed the handkerchief into one of my front pockets. It barely fit. Going down the hill, I kept to the shadows.

The clock struck two.

Chapter Thirty-Five

The train stood dark and still in the moonlight just where it had been the night before, only now there were empty crates and spilled, trampled grapes in the grass and on the ground around it. Crickets chirped and a nighthawk screeched above my head.

"Psst! Over here," said Perks. He was in the shadows beside the barrel where we'd stashed our supplies. "Give me a hand." We pulled off the wrecked pallet and the crate and removed the board that covered the barrel. "Everything's here," said Perks, "only I don't think we need the water now, not if we're riding in the caboose. Caboose has its own water tank. You got the cash?"

I nodded and pulled the wad of money out of my

pocket. "In here," I said. "It's mostly coins." I hoped like anything that Perks wouldn't ask where I'd gotten it.

"I talked Banjo into helping us out," said Perks. "He's already done the deal with Big Swede, agreed on the amount—twenty-six bucks apiece, no questions. All we have to do is be here with the cash at two-thirty. The brakeman knows what's up. We won't even have to talk to Big Swede."

"How much did you tell Banjo?" I asked, feeling nervous and mad and jumpy all at once. "We swore not to tell anyone."

"Hey, it had to be done," said Perks. "You think Big Swede would deal with me? After last year? 'Member, he got a good look, and I got a good kick to my little fanny. I had to get us a middleman on account of circumstances had changed."

"Is he safe?" I asked.

"Yeah, he's safe," said Perks. "Banjo came here on a train when he was twelve himself, hopped it with his uncle and cousins, came all the way from Kentucky, so he ain't one to judge and he won't spill the beans, except he said he'd give Mama the word when we was long gone. He even gave me a silver dollar for good luck." Perks showed me the dollar. It was a brand-new one. "He gave me this, too," said Perks.

"What is it?" I took a small piece of brown paper from Perks. It had a list of names and addresses written in pencil.

"Contacts," said Perks. "This here's Banjo's cousin Donny. He works for the railroad, out of San Francisco. Banjo says if I need a place, or a job, Donny's just like family. His wife is Lily. And there's his uncle Billy. He lives in Los Angeles. Lotta work there, too. There's his other cousin, Simon. He's a preacher, got his own church." Perks folded the paper back up and put it in his pocket. "I never knew Banjo had so many folks in California. Then, of course, there's Bobby Jester, working the Pullman. One thing's for sure. I'm gonna get a new life and a new job, and that's a fact." He rubbed his hands together and grinned.

The clock chimed two-fifteen. Skinny was nowhere in sight.

"I knew Skinny'd chicken," said Perks.

"He said he could get the dough," I said.

"It don't matter," said Perks. "It don't matter one bit. Skinny eats no matter what. Me and you, we have to find our own way."

We sat in the shadows and waited. Every time I heard a noise, I looked to see if it was Skinny, but he never showed. When the clock struck two-thirty, Perks and I stood up, made sure the coast was clear, reached into the barrel and pulled up our gunnysacks, and headed to the end of the grape train. I knocked on the caboose door. The brakeman was waiting.

"Just two?" he said. He was a short, tough-looking bald guy with a mustache as wide as a pocket comb. "Big Swede said there was three." He had an accent. Polish for sure.

"Just two," I said. I gave him the money that wasn't mine, glad to get it out of my hands. Perks handed him his money, wrapped up in brown paper. The bald brakeman smiled.

"I have to count it," he said. We stood there with our gunnysacks and waited until he'd counted out the last penny. "Fifty-two bucks." He nodded and pointed to a large storage locker. "Put your things there," he said. "And you sit there, don't move, and when I say, you climb in, shut the door, and don't make a sound. Got that? Any time the train stops, you hide."

"Got it," I said.

The brakeman pocketed our money and stepped off the caboose. It'd be a tight squeeze. I imagined Matt and Joey stuffed into that locker. How'd they done it? Suddenly I had to pee. I looked at Perks. He was grinning like a fiend. I wished I'd made one last stop at the outhouse.

We sat on the floor beside the locker without talking, our shoulders touching. Time seemed to crawl. I could smell my own sweat, and Perks's, too. The caboose windows were open, but we were sitting too low to see out. A rooster crowed. I wondered about Skinny. Why had he changed his mind? It couldn't have been the money. He'd said he could get it. I thought about the three of us stuffed into the locker and was glad Skinny'd changed his mind. I hoped he'd like Italy.

I heard the crunch of boots on gravel. Perks heard it, too. We both looked at the window and then at each other. Then we scrunched down even closer to the floor.

"You got it?" It was Big Swede's voice.

"Yeah," said the brakeman. I heard the sound of coins and bills being slapped into a palm. It was hard to swallow. I felt desperate for something to drink and now my guts were rumbling. "Only two showed," said the brakeman. "That's twenty-six for you, twenty-six for me."

"Better than nuttin'," said Big Swede. The boots walked away. The rooster crowed again. The clock struck three-fifteen. Ma wouldn't be up for another hour.

There was more talk outside, the sound of foot-steps. The caboose door opened up and the brakeman stepped in. He closed the door, sat at the little table, and rolled a cigarette.

"California, here we come," whispered Perks. His eyes were bright and the smile on his face was as wide as I'd ever seen it. The train whistle blew, one short toot. There was a slight jerk and then the wheels creaked beneath us. Perks wiggled his eyebrows up and down. I tried to smile back but it was a lousy attempt. A cold sweat had broken out on my upper lip, and my heart beat so loud it drowned out everything else. I held my breath and hoped like anything that I could keep myself from puking.

Chapter Thirty-Six

After his cigarette was rolled and lit, the brake-man went outside and stood at the back of the caboose. "Stay down," he said to us before he stepped out. The train crept through Roslyn, tooting at every street it crossed. I counted. The third time the horn sounded I knew we were in Ducktown neighbor-hood. There was one more crossing, one more toot, at the crossing below the hill that led to our house. Would the sound wake Ma? Had she heard it when Matt and Joey left town? The train picked up speed.

"Now we're gonna fly," whispered Perks.

The brakeman came back in, removed his cap, and busied himself at the tiny stove. "You boys want coffee?" he asked.

"Yes, sir," said Perks. "Thank you, sir. I can make

the coffee if you want. I work in a cafe. I can do any kind of work you want, you just say so." The brakeman nodded. Perks jumped up and made himself useful. I didn't move.

I watched from my place on the floor. The train sped up for a while, then when we got to Cle Elum it slowed down again. We crept through the town, and after we crossed the last road, the train picked up more speed.

My palms were slick with sweat and I was breathing hard. I looked up at the window, but from where I was sitting all I could see was the sky filled with stars. We were moving fast, but the stars didn't move at all. It was like they were glued in place, and no matter where the train went, they were up there following and watching.

I'd gotten away without a hitch. I was on my way to Seattle and then on to California, the land of fruit farms and walnut groves and overtime pay. Perks was feeling jolly about the whole thing. Every time he looked my way, he grinned from ear to ear. Why was I feeling sick?

I stared at the sky. No matter where I went, no matter how far I ran, the lying and stealing I'd done, just like the stars in the sky, they'd follow me, watching, hovering over my head, reminding me that I was a crook. It didn't matter if no one else ever knew about it. I knew. I could get away from Roslyn, but I couldn't get away from me.

I needed to puke. "I need some air," I said.

"You're lookin' green," said Perks.

"Out the back," said the brakeman without a glance.

I scrambled up and let myself out the back door. The train swayed from side to side and I had to grab the railing to steady myself. There was a tiny porch at the back of the caboose. I stood there and took in big gulps of air until my gut settled down.

I'd never been on a train before. I'd never ridden on anything this fast before. By afternoon I'd be in Seattle, and in a few days California. It was what I wanted, what I'd planned for, what I'd stolen to be able to do. It was the only way.

Ma'd be waking up soon. Maybe she was already awake, making coffee, stirring the breakfast polenta, and humming to herself. She wouldn't worry about me until Philip let her know I was gone. Then she'd cry for days. I closed my eyes and squeezed them hard.

Inside, I heard Perks laugh.

The caboose leaned to the right as the train pulled around a curve in the track. I looked ahead and even in the darkness, I could make out the bridge over the Cle Elum River. The train slowed down just a bit.

I opened the gate and jumped.

Chapter Thirty-Seven

I hit the tracks and rolled, smacking my left hand so hard that I felt the bones crunch. Perks and the brakeman rushed out the door and started to yell. The brakeman had grabbed the lamp. He held it high. I stood up to show I wasn't hurt, gritting my teeth against the pain in my hand.

"Go on!" I hollered. I gave them the thumbs-up. Perks's mouth was hanging open. My left hand felt like it'd been stepped on by a horse. "Good luck, Perks!" I said. The darkness had swallowed me up. The train was too far away for them to hear me but I yelled anyhow. *"I'm going back!"*

The engine started across the bridge. The brakeman handed the lamp to Perks, shook his head, and went inside. I saw Perks cup one hand around his mouth and yell, *"So long!"*

I stood in the middle of the track and watched until the train was across the river and out of sight. Then I turned around and followed the railroad tracks all the way home to Roslyn.

By the time I got to town, my left hand was twice its normal size and a fine shade of purple. It hurt so bad that I cradled it in my other arm like a baby. My shoulder ached where I'd rolled and I could tell I was going to have a doozy of a bruise on one shin. I was thirsty and hot and the sweat rolled down the sides of my face like drops of rain, but I didn't let it slow me down. I got to Roslyn around nine.

I passed the alley that led up to our house. Ma would read me the riot act when I got home. That much was certain. But I had something to do before I faced her and got what was coming to me. Instead of going straight home, I turned and headed toward the church.

I found Father Duval in the sacristy.

"Dobro jutro, Slava!" Good morning. "I was looking for you yesterday. Did Joseph tell you?" Then he saw my hand. "What is this?"

"I need to make a confession," I said.

"You need the doctor," said Father Duval.

"No, please," I said, my voice squeaking from thirst and tiredness and not a little shame. "This first." I knelt down, wincing on account of the sore leg. Father Duval slipped a stole around his neck and knelt beside me. I crossed myself and whispered, "Bless me, Father, for I have sinned. I stole money." A tear slid down my face.

"Ah," said Father Duval.

"From the collection," I said.

"I see."

There was a long pause. My hand throbbed. I squeezed my eyes shut.

Father Duval spoke. "When a good boy steals, he usually has a reason. . . ." Father's voice was gentle, like he was talking to a little squirt.

"I wanted to go to California. To work."

"...because his mother is about to lose her house, no?"

"How did you—?" I looked up. Father Duval wore a sad smile.

"It is Father's job to know the troubles of his people. How did you hurt your hand?"

"Jumped off the train."

"And you came back to make right what was wrong."

I nodded. The floor was a blur. I wiped my eyes on my shoulders and blinked, waiting for my penance. It would be a big one, a hundred rosaries for the pope's intentions, at least, and a hundred Hail Marys for the poor souls in purgatory. I didn't care. It would never be enough to fix what I'd done.

I swallowed twice and licked my lips. And of course I'd have to pay back all that money. It would take years. Finally Father Duval spoke.

"This is good. Very good, Slava. You have made a good confession. For your penance, say a prayer for all the families less fortunate than your own."

"You don't understand, Father," I said. "The money's gone. I didn't bring it back." Big Swede had half of it, the Polish brakeman had the rest. It might as well have been at the bottom of the ocean.

"Then God can do what He wishes with it, wherever it is."

"It was twenty-six dollars!"

"Twenty-six dollars for a lesson that will last a lifetime?" He shrugged. "It is, as they say, a bargain."

I made the sincerest act of contrition of my life, choking back sobs and wiping my nose on my shoulder like any snot-nosed brat. Say a prayer for the families less fortunate than my own? I'd gotten heavier penances for swearing.

Father Duval said the words of absolution in Latin, but I heard them loud and clear in English. "I absolve thee from thy sins, in the name of the Father, and of the Son, and of the Holy Ghost."

We both said "Amen," and I crossed myself again. Father Duval stood and then helped me up. "Go in peace, Slava. Let your mother know you are safe. Then go see the young doctor. Will you do that?"

"Yes," I said. "I promise." My knees felt like jelly. My whole arm was starting to pound. I took a deep breath. Even though I felt rotten, I felt better. Maybe Ma wouldn't expect too much explanation. And maybe my hurt hand would make her decide against a licking.

"I will call at your house this evening," said Father Duval. He must have seen the look of panic on my face because then he added in a whisper, "What was spoken in confession is absolutely forgotten, yes?" I nodded, unable to say a thing without blubbering. Father Duval put a hand on my shoulder, and when I looked up, he was smiling. "Now I must attend to my duties. There is a funeral at eleven."

Pinky's mom. I'd forgotten. "She was our neighbor," I said.

"I know," said Father Duval. "And now there are seven children without a mother."

"Less fortunate than us?" I said.

Father Duval nodded.

271

Chapter Thirty-Eight

Ma's face went from relieved to mad to happy to upset all in the time it took me to open the back door and step into the kitchen. Her words tumbled out in Croatian.

"Jesus and Mary! Slava! My Slava!" Her hand flew to her heart and she took a step backward.

"Hi-ya, Ma," I said.

"I thought you were gone like your brothers. What are you trying to do, kill me before I'm an old woman? Thanks be to God. Thanks be to God. Look at that hand!" She swiped at a tear and frowned. I bit the inside of my lip as she took my hurt hand and clucked. "Broken," she said. I winced as she turned it over and looked at the palm. Just then Philip came into the kitchen.

"Jeez! Cuss," he said. "You didn't go after all." He grinned and looked at Ma, then at me. Ma pointed at him to get his attention.

"Philip, you go, get the doctor. *Doctor*." He understood and nodded. Then he ran out the door and it slammed shut behind him.

"You sit," said Ma. She poured some water onto a dish towel until it was soaked. Then she wrung the water out into the basin and handed the damp towel to me. "Put this on the hand," she said. Then she poured me a cup of water. I drank it down in two gulps and she poured some more. She sat down across from me.

"I should beat you," she said, "for breaking my heart, for running away. Percy's little sister, she came here looking for him. Then I knew the letter was true, you boys had gone, you and your friend."

"Perks got away," I said. I wondered how far he'd gotten by now. Maybe all the way over the mountains.

"God help us mothers," said Ma. "Our boys can't wait to leave us."

"I didn't want to leave," I said. "I didn't know how else to help."

"I know," said Ma. She patted my good hand and two tears spilled from her eyes and trickled down her cheeks. "If you weren't hurt, I'd skin you alive right now," she said. "Maybe next week." I knew from the look on her face that it would never happen.

Dr. Moody agreed with Ma. "You've broken a bone in your hand," he said. "But we can't do a thing about it until the swelling goes down." He sent Philip down to Slim's for a bucket of chipped ice and made me swallow two aspirin pills. When Ma went into the kitchen to make coffee, Dr. Moody asked for an explanation.

"I jumped off a train," I said.

His eyebrows shot up, but he didn't nose around. "I see," he said. "Anything else hurt?"

I shook my head. The bruise on my shin wasn't any worse than other bruises I'd had.

"Then you were fortunate," said Dr. Moody.

"I know," I said.

Ma wouldn't leave me to go to the funeral, but she sent Philip and gave him a penny and told him to light a candle for her.

Father Duval stopped by after supper. Ma had given me two more aspirin pills and my hand felt a bit better, as long as I didn't move it. Ma showed Father Duval into the house and asked him to sit down.

"How is the patient?" he asked, setting his hat in his lap.

"Fair to middling," I said. "The swelling has gone down some."

"That is good, good," said Father Duval. He cleared his throat and looked at Ma. "I have something to show you, Mrs. Petrovich." He reached into his pocket and drew out two pieces of paper, the same kind we used for school. He unfolded them and I felt my ears turn red. It was my Latin exam.

Father Duval didn't look at me. He handed the exam to Ma and she looked it over. "I don't read too much English," she said.

"This paper, it is written in Latin," said Father Duval. "It was written by Slava. He answered all of the exam questions correctly." Ma nodded and handed it back to the priest. "This part," said Father Duval, pointing to the essay, "is the most important. Slava wrote it himself—two paragraphs."

Ma nodded. Neither of them had looked at me. It was like I wasn't even there.

"There are no mistakes," said Father Duval. I felt a smile creep onto my face.

"Yes, Slava is the smart boy," said Ma. "We speak of this before."

Father Duval reached into his pocket again and pulled out an envelope. He drew out a letter. "Please, allow me to read," he said.

"My Dear Father François:

"It was a distinct pleasure to read the essay by Slava Petrovich. You were correct in your assessment—this is extraordinary work for a boy his age with no previous background in Latin. On your recommendation, and in light of his overall academic excellence as demonstrated in his school records, which you so kindly forwarded to my attention, Saint Martin's Academy wishes to extend a full-tuition scholarship of twenty-five dollars to Master Petrovich for the coming school year.

"Classes begin on the first Monday in September. Please make arrangements for room and board with our high school dean, Father Roger O'Flaherty.

"I will look forward to meeting young Slava. He will make a fine addition to our student body.

"The faculty sends its greetings.

"Sincerely,

"Monsignor Gerard Beaumont, Dean
Saint Martin's Academy High School
and Seminary"

Father Duval put the letter in his lap and looked at me for the first time. He smiled, and I saw that his eyes had the same sparkle I'd noticed on the first day

I'd seen him. I tried to think of something to say, but in the end I was completely tongue-tied. A scholarship? I stared like a dimwit at Father Duval.

"It is wonderful, no?" he said.

"We have no money, nothing," said Ma. She shook her head sadly. "I tell you this before, when you say to let Slava stay in school. His brothers, gone away." She waved with her hand, then dabbed at her eyes with the back of her hand.

"The tuition will be paid," said Father Duval.

"The room and the board we cannot pay," said Ma.

"That has been taken care of," said Father Duval, grinning in my direction. "There is a benefactor, a friend who wishes to remain anonymous. Please, Mrs. Petrovich," he said. "Slava has a gift, a treasure. It would be a sin to waste it."

I bit the inside of my cheek to make sure I wasn't dreaming. The pain told me what I wanted to know. I wasn't dreaming. I was wide, wide awake. The Dean of Saint Martin's had read my Latin essay, and now he wanted me at his school. Suddenly it hit me between the eyes like a cannonball. A wild feeling of hope filled me up so fast that I thought I might explode.

"He don't want to be a priest," said Ma. "I already ask."

"Boys his age don't know what they want," said Father Duval. "If he doesn't finish school, he could miss his calling." He glanced in my direction and winked. Ma folded and unfolded her hands a couple of times.

"Slava," she said, switching to Croatian, "tell me the truth. Do you want to go to boarding school?" I felt like someone had just pointed to a mountain of gold bricks and asked if I'd like to have a few. I took a deep breath. I looked Ma right in the eye.

"I want to work," I said in English, so Father Duval would be able to understand, too. I held my breath. I waited, listening to hear my only chance at my dream of high school be smashed into a thousand little bits.

"Father," said Ma with a sigh, "this boy, he lies so much. Many time I tell him to lie is a sin, but he don't listen. At the school they teach him not to lie, yes? Hokey-dokey. He goes."

"But—" I started to speak, but Ma interrupted.

"I have decided," she said, and then she turned to Father Duval. "Please, you take him. God will provide. Maybe Slava is priest someday."

"Perhaps," said Father Duval. He was grinning from ear to ear. When I looked at Ma, she was smiling, too. Father Duval stood up and put on his hat. "I will send a telegram today to inform the monsignor that you are coming," he said, and then he tipped his hat at me. "You have only one week to get ready. *Laku noć,* my friends."

"*Laku noć,*" Ma and I said together.

As soon as the door closed behind Father Duval, I let out a whoop and a holler that I could swear reached all the way to California.

Chapter Thirty-Nine

Even though I was happy enough to sprout wings and fly, I couldn't stop thinking about how Ma expected to make ends meet with me away at school. Every time I mentioned it, she shut me up in a hurry. "Don't talk to me about money," she said. But how would she and Philip get by? Where would they live? I didn't know, and Ma wouldn't say a word.

Ma also wouldn't let me lift a finger for another whole day, so I sat on my fanny and reread an old copy of the *Miner's Echo* and tried to ignore the ants in my pants. I was going to school! But what about the house?

Skinny came by. Mary'd seen him at the butcher shop and had told him about my broken hand and how I'd lost Matt's boots and a good shirt and the poetry book she'd given me for my birthday. Skinny brought me a stack of *National Geographic*s to pass the time.

"It's all of this year's magazines up to July," he said. "We've read them already."

I thumbed through the April issue. There were pictures and articles and even a map. "Thanks, pal," I said. I missed my poetry book, but the *National Geographic*s were first-rate.

I showed Skinny my hand. The swelling had gone down, but it was still black and blue. "Dr. Moody is going to splint it today," I said. "Then I can do something besides sit like a sack of potatoes."

"I heard you're going to Saint Martin's Academy," said Skinny.

"Yeah. I got a full scholarship."

"That's swell for you, Cuss," said Skinny. "Glad it ain't me. I'm quitting school, myself."

"On account of going back to Italy?" I said.

Skinny shook his head. "Pop changed his mind. That's why I didn't show up at the train. I bet you boys thought I was chicken."

"Yeah, that's what we thought, all right," I said, smiling so he'd know I didn't hold it against him.

"Ma cried for days until Pop said he'd give it one more year. He let go Luigi, the other butcher, and said I can work full-time. He's gonna change the sign to read 'Giombetti and Son.' If we can make it this year, no Italy."

"Perks got clean away," I said. "I bet a nickel he's in California by now."

"I bet another nickel he'll find work right off," said Skinny, "knowing him."

"You should've seen his list," I said. "Uncles, cousins, friends of friends, even a colored preacher who has his own church. Somebody'll hire him, and he'll do any work they give him."

"Perks has a ton of spunk," said Skinny.

"Yeah," I said, and in my mind I imagined my best pal all grown up and sitting behind the wheel of a shiny new Ford sedan. "He does for certain."

Dr. Moody splinted my left hand just before supper. It was tender but I could already tell it was better than before. I was glad it wasn't my right hand. I'd need it for school. "This will keep the bone in place," the doctor said. "You'll need to wear it for a month, and then you can take it off. Try to keep it clean and dry. Wiggle your fingers throughout the day."

"I'm going to Saint Martin's Academy," I said. "The train leaves Friday morning."

"I heard," said Dr. Moody, concentrating on wrapping the splints up tight. "Do you plan to tell your teachers how proficient you are in those—what is it?—fourteen languages?" He grinned without looking up and I felt my ears turn hot.

"I'll just tell them about Croatian and Latin," I said. "Father Duval says they teach French and German on top of Latin."

"I'm sure you'll discover some colorful new expressions," said Dr. Moody. He messed up my hair and then he opened his bag and pulled out a small package. "I ordered this for Philip some weeks back and it just arrived today. I hope he enjoys it."

I took the package from the doctor and laid it on the table. Philip was out in back, kicking a ball around in the dirt. "Want me to get him?" I asked.

"Oh, no," said Dr. Moody. "Don't bother. He'll have plenty of time to look at it later. Goodbye. I'll check on you at least once more before Friday."

I waved with my good hand. I was leaving Roslyn, really and truly. It was hard to believe.

The next couple of days were normal enough, except that I couldn't do a lick of work with my hand in a splint. Mary and Hairy came by and gave me a package of six brand-new pencils, a whole ream of writing paper, and a gum eraser.

"They're grand, aren't they?" said Mary, patting baby Walter on the back until he let out a belch any uncle would be proud of.

"Yeah, thanks," I said.

"You'd better be careful with all that reading, though," said Mary, pointing at the stack of *National Geographic*s on the table. "Too much and you'll need specs."

I grinned and Mary laughed and Ma put on the kettle. Ma asked them to stay for supper and we had a dandy time despite the meager fixings. Mary chatted about the baby, while Hairy smoked and smiled and showed Philip how to play solitaire.

Ma laughed out loud more than once at Mary's gossip, and after supper she rocked Walter to sleep. Ma seemed happier than I'd seen her in a long time. Even though she didn't want to talk about money, I couldn't get it out of my head. What would Ma and Philip do when the bank took the house away?

I counted down the days.

Ma darned all my socks and got out my wool jacket. "Too small," she said, then took down the sleeves. My aunts came by with hand-me-downs: three pairs of wool trousers, two white shirts, and a half-dozen undershirts. I didn't tell Ma that my other clothes were somewhere on a train to California, and she didn't ask. Aunt Katja gave me a brand-new hand-kerchief and one of Uncle Tony's bow ties, plus a pair of real shoes, scuffed and down at the heels, but better than any boots I owned and not as old-fashioned as Pa's shoes.

"Uncle Tony, he don't want you looking cheap," said Aunt Katja in her heavy accent. I thanked her and she gave me a hug. "All of us is proud of Slava."

It was the night before I was supposed to leave. My excitement over going away to school was mixed with anxiousness over Ma and Philip and I couldn't sleep a wink. I went downstairs and found Ma alone, sitting at the kitchen table. "Please, Ma," I said in Croatian. "I have to know how you are going to get by." This time she didn't shut me up.

"Lose the house, so what?" She shrugged and smiled. "It's only a house."

I took a deep breath and then I spilled my guts. "I wrote to Matt and Joey," I said. "I know where they are. I wrote to the farm. I didn't use their names." Ma stared. I kept on going. I needed to get everything off my chest. "I told them about Philip getting sick and being deaf, and how you spent all your money on doctors. I told them that you mortgaged the house, and I told them how much you owed. I told them not to come back, I told them about . . . the fellows who died, the bootlegging troubles."

I looked at my feet. My toenails needed cleaning. No boy at boarding school would have dirty toenails.

"I thought they should know, Ma. They love you. Like all of us. Like me."

Ma reached over and patted my cheek. "You boys, you boys. You make me happy and you break my heart, but all the time I know you love me. No more worrying, Slava Petrovich. You should not have written. Now they will worry, too." Ma thought for a minute and then she shrugged and smiled. "What is done, is done. We shall see what comes of it."

"Ma, you need money!" I said. "I'm leaving tomorrow. Who'll earn wages for you?" My voice squeaked and my eyes watered up.

"Slava, I have six sisters and two brothers in this town. Have you forgotten? We came here together, on the same ship across the ocean, on the same train across this country. Do you think they will let me starve?" I shook my head. "I will not let them help me, of course," said Ma, sounding like her old self, "but just in case, they are here.

"Besides," said Ma, "more than a year ago, Mrs. Szabo at the boardinghouse asked me to work full-time as a washerwoman, but part of the pay was a room, and what good did that do me when I had my own house? Soon," said Ma, "I will need a place to live. And I know she needs a washerwoman because I am doing all the wash as it is! If I live there, she pays me less, but I have a roof. I can keep my cows in the boardinghouse stables. It is all arranged today, this morning. The room at the boardinghouse is big enough only for me, and one little boy, too. So you see? God provides. You go away to school, and I will have a place to live. Philip, too. If you don't go to school, we will have no place to live."

I let this news soak in, and in a few seconds I started to feel like a man who'd been let out of jail. I tried not to act too happy.

"Tough luck about the house," I said, looking around at the only home I'd ever known.

"Another day I will have another house," said Ma. "This is America."

"And you have decided," I said, imitating her thick accent. Ma laughed and tweaked my nose and then she gave me a big hug.

Chapter Forty

We went down to the train station in the dark. Philip tagged along, carrying some of the food our aunts had brought over. Father Duval met us there. He took my suitcase and handed it to the porter. Skinny showed up, out of breath and waving a big pepperoni in his hand.

"You'll need this," he said. "And I didn't swipe it. Ma sent it for you."

I shook hands with my pal. "Tell her thanks," I said. "And have fun being a butcher."

"Have fun being a schoolboy," said Skinny. "I'm just glad it ain't me."

A schoolboy. It was true. I pulled at my collar and straightened Uncle Tony's bow tie. The whistle blew and the conductor yelled, "All aboard!"

Father Duval handed me my ticket. Then he blessed me and told me to write. "I want to hear everything!" he said.

I promised to write. Then I said goodbye.

Ma hugged me.

"*Volim te,*" I whispered in her ear. *I love you.* I smacked Philip in the arm. He grinned and held his hand up in a fist, and then he made some funny moves with his fingers.

"I just said 'so long' in finger spelling," said Philip. "It's in a book Dr. Moody gave me. It's a way to talk to deaf people. I'm gonna teach Ma."

"You're a swell little squirt," I said, and I'm pretty sure he understood. He grinned and I messed up his hair. I was going to miss him. I was going to miss them all. I made my way up the steps into the train.

"Slava, wait!" It was Father Duval. "Something for you." He handed me a small, heavy cardboard box. "Now be on your way!"

I found a seat and pulled down the window.

"Goodbye!" I yelled.

"*Bog bio s tobom!*" said Ma, then threw me a kiss. *God go with you.*

The train whistle blew again and the train pulled out of the station. I waved until my family and friends were out of sight.

The box was on my lap. I undid the strings and opened the flaps. I looked into the box and let out a whistle. Inside was a brand-new, leather-bound copy of *Gray's Anatomy*.

I lifted out the big book and opened the front cover. There, in scrawly writing, was an inscription. I translated it without a hitch. A big grin spread across my face.

Slava: Utinam vocationem veram invenis!
Amicus carus,
Donald Moody, M.D.

To Slava: May you find your true calling!
Your friend,
Donald Moody, M.D.

Ten miles later I was still smiling.

Slava est nomen mihi. Ego sum puer. Tredecim annos habeo. Tempore brevi vir ero. Vir laborat et cubum effert. Vir de se non cogitat. Puer multa cupit dum vir non multa vult. Vir id quod justum est agit, etiamsi est difficile.

Nec pater nec mater in schola studuit. Ego septem annos in schola studui. Plus eruditionem quam aliquis in familia habeo. Linguam Latinam legere possum. In Latina doctior esse volo, sed necesse est agere quod est justum. Multum est septem annos studere. Fortunatissimus sum.

My name is Slava. I am a boy. I am thirteen years old. Soon I will be a man. A man works and provides food. He does not think about himself. A boy wishes for many things, while a man does not. A man does what is right, even if it is difficult.

Neither my father nor my mother went to school. I have studied in school for seven years. I have more education than anyone in my family. I can read Latin. I wish to learn more Latin, but I must do what is right. Seven years of school is a lot. I am very fortunate.

My father was born and raised in Roslyn, Washington. A few years ago he told me about the grape train that came once a year to their little town, loaded with wine grapes from California. He said most boys tried to steal grapes off the train and that it was a fun but dangerous business. Dad told me other stories from his childhood, and I asked a lot of questions. Soon I realized that I had to write a book. All I knew for sure was that the story would have to include three elements: the grape train, boys with nicknames, and lots of nighttime shenanigans.

I spent a week doing research in Roslyn. I hung out in the museum and took notes while the curator told me about the old days. I studied in the library, which was only open for three hours each day. I sat in the barbershop and listened as Jerry the barber explained how often it was necessary to move an outhouse and how to mix up sulfur salve. I wandered around town, snooped in the churches, explored

Kristine Franklin's grandmother, Uljana Brozovich, posing with three of her eight children. Left to right: Luke, Olga, and the author's father, Steve.

abandoned coal mines and climbed slag heaps, threw pinecones in the Cle Elum River, and read hundreds of yellowed pages of the *Miner's Echo*. When I was ready, I began to write.

Cuss is a work of fiction. All the characters were born in my imagination, but here and there the book *does* include bits and pieces of my family history. I had an uncle Slava who went by the nickname "Hap." My great-uncle Tony was famous for his homemade slivovitz. My grandmother fed sauerkraut juice to sick children, and although she lived in America for more than sixty years, she never liked to speak English. My grandfather was a coal miner; so were my older uncles. My father loved to read. One year his sister Mary gave him a book of poems as a gift. It was his first book. Eighty years later, he still has it.

—Kristine Louise Brozovich Franklin

ACKNOWLEDGMENTS

The author wishes to acknowledge the generous help of the following people: Mary Andler of the Roslyn Museum; Erin Krake of the Roslyn Public Library; Joe Lowatchie, former coal miner; Jerry Morris, barber and storyteller par excellence; Mona Risser and Jack Stoner of the *North Kittitas County Tribune;* all the citizens of Roslyn, Washington, who helped me with my research; Frank Nolte, who taught me about life as an altar boy; Patrick Krason, who translated the French phrases; Gun Edberg Caldwell, who contributed the Swedish insults; Kris McKusky, Jared Copeland, and Fr. Clem Gustin, O.S.C., who helped me with the Latin; and, most especially, Anna Marie Hosticka, who not only translated numerous words and phrases into Croatian, but also connected me to the culture and faith of my father's people.

To each of you a very hearty *Hvala!*

WHEN YOU THINK YOU'VE LOST EVERYONE,
YOU DON'T WANT TO NEED ANYONE.

Lone Wolf
by Kristine L. Franklin

Three years ago, Perry Dubois and his dad left their lives
behind and moved to the north woods. They don't see
other people much up there. Perry's dad likes it that way,
and Perry is getting used to it, too. So when Willow
Pestalozzi and her large family move in nearby, Perry's
not all that happy about it. Still, he can't help being drawn
in by the warmth of the Pestalozzis' household—even if
it reminds him of everything he wants to forget.

"Strong characters, a plot that works on many levels, and
an engaging background make this *Wolf* a standout."

—*School Library Journal*

Paperback ISBN 978-0-7636-2996-0

ALSO BY KRISTINE L. FRANKLIN

Dove Song

Bobbie Lynn's mother has always been dependent on Daddy for everything. Now Daddy has been sent away to the war in Vietnam, and Bobbie Lynn is worried. So is her older brother, Mason. How is Mama going to take care of them without Daddy's help for a whole year? And what if Daddy never comes home at all?

"A moving novel about friendship and responsibility that is at once sorrowful and joyful." —*Booklist*

"Both a sensitive story of friendship and family problems and solid historical fiction."
                                   —*School Library Journal*

Paperback ISBN 978-0-7636-3219-9